Kung Fu Princess 1

Daughter of Light

KUNG FU PRINCESS 1

DAUGHTER OF LIGHT

WRITTEN BY PAMELA WALKER

GROSSET & DUNLAP
A PARACHUTE PRESS BOOK

I would like to offer my deepest thanks to Grandmaster Frank DeMaria, founder of the American Center for Chinese Studies, for reading the manuscript draft and offering his encouragement and guidance. Much appreciation also to Kurtis Carter for allowing me the use of his extensive library on martial arts.

∂∂∂∂∂

GROSSET & DUNLAP
Published by the Penguin Group
Penguin Group (USA) Inc., 375 Hudson Street, New York, New York 10014, U.S.A.
Penguin Group (Canada), 90 Eglinton Avenue East, Suite 700, Toronto, Ontario,
Canada M4P 2Y3 (a division of Pearson Penguin Canada Inc.)
Penguin Books Ltd, 80 Strand, London WC2R 0RL, England
Penguin Ireland, 25 St Stephen's Green, Dublin 2, Ireland
(a division of Penguin Books Ltd)
Penguin Group (Australia), 250 Camberwell Road, Camberwell, Victoria 3124,
Australia (a division of Pearson Australia Group Pty Ltd)
Penguin Books India Pvt Ltd, 11 Community Centre, Panchsheel Park,
New Delhi -110 017, India
Penguin Group (NZ), Cnr Airborne and Rosedale Roads, Albany, Auckland 1310,
New Zealand (a division of Pearson New Zealand Ltd)
Penguin Books (South Africa) (Pty) Ltd, 24 Sturdee Avenue, Rosebank,
Johannesburg 2196, South Africa
Penguin Books Ltd, Registered Offices:
80 Strand, London WC2R 0RL, England

Cover and interior design by Rosanne S. Guararra
Cover photograph by David Mager/Pearson Learning Group

Library of Congress Control Number: 2006002181

ISBN 0-448-44139-X   10 9 8 7 6 5 4 3 2 1

The Prophecy

A daughter of light,

Blood of Ng Mui and Yim Wing Chun,

Will be born into the power of her ancestors,

Born to finish the battles they began.

In her fourteenth year her destiny will unfold:

Through five gold coins, each death or strength.

Her ancestors' enemies will seek her,

The demons and ghosts will gather,

But in gold and jade, she will find her gifts,

And the veil of secrets will open to her.

 Chapter One

Cassidy Chen ran through the dark gloom of the forest, her heart beating out the warning to flee in a pulsing sound track that throbbed in her ears. Her throat burned in that raw, scorched way that running from danger brings. Just ahead she spotted a large tree that reached out to the sky with limbs like thick arms. Go there. The words were clear in her head and as soon as she thought them, she was at the ancient tree, one foot on the rough, gray bark of the trunk, leaping up to the first branch, then the next and the next, until finally she was hidden high in its dense, sheltering foliage. How did that happen? she wondered. I practically flew up here!

She heard an inhuman hiss below that caused her spine to stiffen in fear. Pushing aside the dark leaves, she could hardly believe what she saw. At the foot of the tree stood the most grotesque and frightening creature she had ever seen. The creature appeared to be part man and part snake. He peered at her up through the thick tangle of branches and leaves. Cassidy watched in horror as he reached toward the first branch with a powerful arm and pulled himself up by coiling the lower half of his body around the trunk of the tree. She was filled with a sick panic that made her pulse race. She looked up to the next branch but knew that she couldn't reach it. The man-snake, red with anger, lifted his head and reached high up into the tree to the thick, mossy branch where Cassidy stood, paralyzed with fear. As his hand wrapped around the branch, she saw with horror that each finger was a long, thin snake. Their dark heads leaped toward Cassidy, mouths open and silvery forked tongues licking the air. Cassidy felt the finger-snakes on the monster's hand wrap around her ankles and sink their tiny, daggerlike fangs into her legs. The poison burned like acid, and Cassidy could feel her blood begin to sizzle in her veins and spread through her body. She took a deep breath and looked up through the lacy leaves of the tree toward a storm-gray sky. There was nowhere to go.

"Wake up, birthday girl!" Cassidy's mother called up the stairs.

"Not yet," Cassidy mumbled. "I'm still sleeping." She tried to move her legs but felt a warm heaviness — a paralysis, maybe — and remembered her dream. Opening her eyes, she found Monty, her ginger cat, stretching his long, chunky body across her feet.

"I'm awake, Mom," Cassidy called in a definitely less-than-excited voice. "I'll be down in a minute."

Cassidy grabbed her journal and jotted down as much of the dream as she could remember. *Okay, so maybe I've been watching too many movies,* she thought. She riffled through the pages and noticed a recurring theme. *Chased into a cave by a rat as large as a horse, ran from a monster that had a hundred arms and two heads, pursued by a pack of blood-spitting coyotes.*

Why am I always running from some weird creature? she wondered.

Cassidy snapped the cover closed on her dark blue dream journal and returned it to the drawer of her nightstand. She crawled out of bed. Why couldn't her school have a birthday policy like her dad's company, where the employees were encouraged to take their birthday off to do whatever they wanted? "So what do all you crazy software engineers do on your birthdays?" she had asked her dad on his birthday in August.

"Well, this one plans to mow the lawn and then do a little weeding," he had answered. That was her dad, Mr. Practical. Her mother would have found a much more interesting way to spend a day off work from the Happy Bunny Preschool. Probably rock climbing or getting a henna tattoo.

"Hey! Nobody's getting any younger down here," her mother called again.

๑๑๑๑๑

"I was going to make birthday muffins this morning," Cassidy's mother said once Cassidy made it down to the breakfast room, "but I'm running late. June called in sick, and I've got to get down to the Happy Bunny. They're up to their necks in little people this morning. Namely Sebastian and his penchant for finger painting on the walls." Sebastian was one of her mother's biggest "handfuls."

"No worries," Cassidy said with laugh. "I'm happy to get a ride with Eliza if that's any help."

"And how will you get home?"

"I've got Wing Chun class this afternoon, so I'll take the bus downtown," Cassidy reminded her mother. Wing Chun was a type of kung fu developed hundreds of years ago.

"Super—that all works out fine," Wendy Chen said, and began fluffing her hair in the mirror.

Thankfully, Cassidy's mom didn't know that Eliza Clifford's mother was secretly referred to as the

Queen of Fender Benders.

"But make sure you come straight home after class because Dad and I are taking you out for a birthday dinner."

After another quick look in the mirror, Wendy Chen pursed her lips into a peachy pink bow, then gave her daughter a final peck on the cheek. She caught sight of their reflections standing side by side in the mirror.

"Look at the two of us!" her mom said. "We're almost the same height. And you just keep getting more beautiful every year."

Once her mom left, Cassidy looked at herself in the mirror. Was she really beautiful? Maybe all mothers said that. Cassidy was so used to seeing the same face, it was hard for her to tell. Most of her looks came from her father, who was Chinese—straight black hair and a short, somewhat broad nose. But her jade green eyes came from her mother, who was Irish. Cassidy turned sideways and wasn't surprised to find that except for a somewhat pudgy tummy, her figure was still as depressingly straight as the day before. "Hello, gorgeous body, are you in there?"

After two years studying with Master Lau, she was still pretty far away from having the willowy, athletic figure she dreamed of. And she was nowhere near flying soundlessly through the air like the characters in her favorite movie, *Crouching Tiger,*

Hidden Dragon. Of course, that was just a movie.

Cassidy assumed the fierce fighting stance of a warrior and observed her reflection. *Not bad*, she thought. Her hand was in the correct position, poised properly at the center of her chest. She thrust it forward rapidly and then retracted it to the chambered position back at the center of her chest. *Master Lau would approve*, she thought.

Monty, Cassidy's cat, rubbed his head against her ankle. *Enough about you*, he seemed to be saying. *It's time to give me some attention now.* He took an impressive flying leap from the floor to the kitchen counter, then landed without a sound, reaching out a soft paw to Cassidy. "I wish I could do that, you lucky cat," Cassidy told him. She fixed herself a bowl of cereal and picked up the phone to call her best friend, Eliza.

Five rings and still no answer—which probably meant that the Cliffords had lost their cordless phone again. While Cassidy waited for the lost phone to be found, she walked to the front window and looked down the long drive to the street.

The mist, just beginning to burn away in the rare presence of Seattle sunshine, partially hid a dark figure. Fog had softened the edges of everything on the street, but Cassidy was certain that someone or something was out there.

She looked closer now and saw an older man standing near the Chens' mailbox. He looked toward the house and then back down the street, as if he wasn't quite sure he was at the right place. Cassidy noticed that he held something small and square in his hand. He glanced down at the object and then peered up the steep drive toward the house where Cassidy stood at the tall front windows.

Cassidy wasn't sure that he saw her, but he paused for a moment and then stepped back into a thicker pocket of fog as if he suddenly realized that he was being watched. She couldn't even see his outline now in the heavy mist that swirled along the drive and sidewalk, and Cassidy wondered for a minute if he had ever really been there.

At last, Ms. Clifford answered the phone, out of breath and yelling to Eliza that she'd found it.

"Hi, Ms. Clifford, it's Cassidy. Could I catch a ride to school with you and Eliza today?"

"Sure, Cassidy, we'll be there in about half an hour."

"Thanks," Cassidy said. She looked out the window again, but there was no sign of the man she'd seen down at the sidewalk. *Probably a tourist who took a wrong turn,* she thought. Seattle tourists were famous for losing their way and finding themselves on Cassidy's street instead of down by the bridge, where a huge cement troll watched over the neighborhood with its single chrome eye. When Cassidy was younger, her mother told her the story of the Three Billy Goats Gruff, and Cassidy had always pictured the huge, shaggy head of the monster peering over the edge of the Aurora Bridge, his angry chrome eye shining as he searched for trespassers.

After a quick shower, Cassidy dressed in her standard uniform of loose jeans and a sweatshirt. This one was pink, with a faded *Mr. Bubbles* logo. It was one of the many funky sweatshirts she'd bought at Tootie's Vintage Tees in Fremont.

While Cassidy waited out on the sidewalk for her ride, a cool drizzle, something between a mist and actual rain, began to fall. *Come on, come on!* Cassidy willed the Cliffords to appear before she had to run back to the house to keep from getting completely soaked. She looked to her right and saw dim yellow headlights appear out of the gloom, but then the car made a left onto a side street. *Wasn't the sun out before? Crazy Seattle weather,* she thought. *I might as well wait inside.*

Cassidy turned, and there was the man she'd seen earlier at the end of their driveway. *Was he waiting here the entire time?* Too startled to speak, she looked at him, and then instinct, or perhaps some training from her kung fu instructor, Master Lau, told her to take a step back. Cassidy wondered if the man had been watching the house, or maybe he had seen that her mother had already left for the morning. She felt a quickening of her pulse and stood ready—though for what, she wasn't sure. *Maybe ready to run,* she thought, remembering her many dreams.

The man didn't speak but lowered his eyes and bowed his head slightly, as if to say she had no reason to be afraid. His hair, mostly gray, had a streak of pure white that fell across his forehead when he looked down. He pushed it from his face and then held out a package wrapped in brown paper, the words *For the daughter of Simon Chen* scrawled across it.

Cassidy took the package and then glanced up to ask, "Who sent this?" But the man was gone. She looked down the sidewalk and thought she saw the back of his white shirt as he walked away, then a slight breeze pulled in a thicker swirl of mist and she couldn't see anything. *But he was just here!* Cassidy thought, and looked at the package in her hands. *Who was that guy?*

The blare of a horn announced the arrival of Eliza Clifford and her mother.

"Sorry we're late!" Eliza called through the open window.

"It was just one thing after another this entire morning," Sarah Clifford said. "But we're here now."

"That's okay," said Cassidy. "I don't think we'll be that late."

As they peeled away from the curb in the

Cliffords' banged-up Toyota, Eliza sang "Happy Birthday" in a loud, off-key voice. Cassidy looked down the sidewalk to see if she could spot the stranger who had given her the package. There was no sign of him anywhere. It was as if he had simply dissolved into the foggy September morning of her fourteenth birthday.

❧ Chapter Two

In the backseat of the car, Cassidy examined the small brown package. She was eager to open it but just as eager to make it to her next birthday. Reluctantly she put the package in her backpack and concentrated on sending safe thoughts to Eliza's mother.

❧❧❧❧❧

The first warning bell sounded just as Cassidy and Eliza ran through the middle school's front door. They had ten minutes to go to their lockers and then get to morning assembly in the gym.

"Do you think I've got time to pick up another permission slip for cheerleader tryouts?" Eliza asked. "I've lost the form, and I have to turn it in tomorrow."

"Yeah, if you hurry," Cassidy said. "I'll meet you in the gym."

All around Cassidy, students lined the hallway, pulling books and papers out of lockers, checking their hair in stick-on mirrors inside the metal, vented doors. At her locker, Cassidy took out her textbooks for her first- and second-period classes. She reached into the outer pocket of her backpack and pulled out the mysterious package. Was there enough time to open it? A quick glance at the clock showed she had seven minutes. *I've got to open it now,* she thought. *Otherwise I'll have to wait until lunch.*

In the library Mrs. Marcum was busy putting spine labels on a stack of books. Cassidy took a quick look around and saw no other students. *Perfect,* she thought.

She loved the quiet coolness of the library. It was in the older part of the school and had somehow escaped the modernization that the rest of the building had undergone. It still had its original wide plank floors that hadn't yet been covered up by drab, olive green tiles. The dark oak shelves were lined with colorful books, and one wall contained nothing but long windows that stretched from ceiling to floor.

Cassidy hurried to a table near one of the windows and out of the view of Mrs. Marcum. She took the package from her backpack and set it on the table. *For the daughter of Simon Chen.* The words were written in small squared-off letters. *Strange way to address a gift,* she thought. *Why wouldn't someone just write:* To Cassidy Chen?

She saw that the brown paper had been folded so that the corners were tucked into each other, forming small triangles on the underside, each point tucked into another triangle. The edges of the paper had been creased sharply, and the box had been completely wrapped and secured without one single piece of tape. As she slid her finger under one of the folds along the back, the paper fell away from a wooden box carved with an elaborate design of tangled branches and leaves. The top of the box fit snugly over the bottom, and Cassidy had some difficulty opening it. She wondered if it had been a long time since the box had been opened. Inside was a slip of rice paper, yellowed and thin as gossamer. Two lines, handwritten in thick black ink, read:

For Mingmei Chen on her 14th birthday.
You must use these well.

Mingmei Chen? That's not my name. Was it possible that she had just opened a gift that was meant for someone else? *Is there some other Simon Chen who has a daughter named Mingmei?* Cassidy thought about it. *Could be,* she thought, *but what are the odds that this Mingmei is also having a birthday on September 6?*

Cassidy took out the slip of rice paper and saw that below the note were five gold coins, each of them somewhat larger than a quarter and much heavier. They looked positively ancient. Cassidy had never seen anything like them before. They were much thicker than ordinary coins, and the gold gleamed in the sunlight that poured through the library window. *This can't be real gold, can it?* she wondered. She didn't recognize any of the Chinese letters or symbols on the coins, not that she knew that much about what really old Chinese coins looked like.

One by one, she examined them. Each was engraved with an intricate design. One coin seemed to show a coiled rope, or was it a snake? There was definitely a coil of some kind that seemed to disappear into the center of the coin. Cassidy rubbed her finger over the second coin. Wavy lines, she decided—one long wavy line and several smaller ones. The third coin was an animal of some type. She could see a pointed nose and sharp ears and thought that it might be a dog or a fox.

The fourth coin showed a woman holding a sword in her left hand. The fifth coin was the hardest to figure out. Cassidy turned it around and around several times and finally decided that it was engraved with a circle of openmouthed faces that ringed the outer edge.

If the gift was really meant for her and not somebody named Mingmei, then who would give her something like this? Was it possible that she had a Chinese name? She'd always thought that the name Cassidy was some old family name on her mother's side—so it was possible, she guessed, that Mingmei could be some name from her father's side of the family. But if that was true, then who, besides her mom and dad, would even know about it?

A glance at the school clock near the double library doors told her that she had about two minutes to get to the gym for morning assembly. With much care and attention, Cassidy put the coins back in the box and placed the rice paper note on top. The lid of the box was a tight fit, but at last she was able to slide it down over the bottom of the box. She put everything in her backpack, which she slung over her shoulder.

A rush of students heading to the gym for assembly pulled Cassidy along in its wake.

Moments later Eliza waved to Cassidy from one of the top bleachers on the eighth-grade side. "Hey, Cass, up here!" Eliza called.

The morning thunder of hundreds of students filing into the gymnasium echoed around the freshly painted walls and steel girders that crisscrossed the ceiling.

Cassidy started up the concrete steps that led to the upper bleachers. She had almost reached Eliza on the top row when the steps seemed to waver and then dissolve right before her eyes. Cassidy suddenly felt as if she were teetering at the edge of a dark and bottomless pit. She heard a loud hissing and rattling sound below her, and she smelled the damp, musty odor of a cave.

Then she saw the snakes — hundreds of snakes intertwined, boiling in the pit below her. They were thick-bodied, and their blunt heads thrust forward, trying to reach her at the edge of the abyss. Her mind screamed, *No!* but her throat felt frozen, allowing no sound to escape. The jagged edge of the pit began to break away beneath her feet.

She pitched forward and brought the palms of both hands down hard on the concrete steps of the bleachers. The jolt sent a shock of pain through her wrists and arms all the way up to her shoulders.

"You okay?" Eliza asked, moving toward Cassidy.

What just happened? Cassidy blinked a few times to clear her eyes. *The floor just kind of melted away and then opened up to a pit of snakes! But that's crazy! I must have caught my toe on the step.* She looked back at the steps, ordinary gray concrete, dingy and scuffed, littered with gum wrappers and a broken pencil. *Snakes? I actually thought I saw snakes?*

She glanced around to see who else had just witnessed her supreme act of klutziness. Fortunately, only Eliza had seen her near-fall. Other students were busy sliding into seats and talking to each other.

Cassidy sat down and shrugged the backpack off her shoulder. She held her palms open for inspection. They were red and scuffed, dotted with tiny pinpoints of blood. "Yeah, I'm fine," she said, rubbing her palms together. "I think I got a little dizzy or something. I don't know, the floor kind of looked — *weird*."

Mr. Edwards, the Cleary Street Middle School principal, thumped the microphone clipped to the podium. When nothing happened, he followed the wires to the sound box.

Around the gym, the students talked and laughed, taking advantage of the delay.

"And speaking of weird," Cassidy said, reaching into her backpack and pulling out the box of coins, "my whole morning started out really freaky." She handed the package to Eliza.

"So, I'm standing on the sidewalk, waiting for you," Cassidy said as Eliza slipped the carved top from the box, "when this man just sort of appears, hands me this package, and then — leaves — without saying a word. He's there one minute and the next he's gone."

"Like a FedEx guy?" Eliza asked, peering into the box.

"No, a stranger," Cassidy told her. "I've never

seen him before."

"Who's Mingmei?" Eliza asked as she examined the note.

"No idea," Cassidy said, shrugging.

Eliza turned the coins over in her hand. "Definitely weird," she said, looking at them closely. "Do you think you have a secret admirer?"

Before Cassidy could answer, an electronic squawk from the sound system filled the gym with a long, piercing screech. Everyone, teachers included, clapped their hands over their ears and winced in pain. Mr. Edwards scrambled quickly across the floor and attempted to find the volume control on the sound panel.

As Eliza continued to inspect the coins, Cassidy glanced back at the solid concrete steps that had seemed to dissolve into nothingness just moments before. *It really was like a pit,* she thought, *a pit of snakes that I almost fell into!* As strange as the episode was, Cassidy didn't want to overthink it. *I'm probably just tired. Maybe I didn't sleep very well last night. Maybe I had other bad dreams, but I only remember that last one because it was right before I woke up.*

✿✿✿✿✿

As the last bell of the day sounded, Cassidy and the other eighth-graders spilled out the school doors.

Cassidy walked down the sidewalk toward the bus stop with Eliza. "Are you off to Hip Hop?" Cassidy asked her.

"Yeah," Eliza said. "I wish my mom would get here already. There's this one cute guy in the class, Ben something or other. I want to get there early enough to stand next to him during the warm-up. You guys celebrating your birthday tonight?"

"Yeah, Café Jones, I think," Cassidy said.

"Ooh, love Café Jones!" Eliza said, and then looked toward the street. "I gotta go—there's my mom! Have fun, Cass, and happy birthday again!"

After Eliza and her mom pulled away from the curb, Cassidy waited at the corner for the downtown bus that would take her to Master Lau's Wing Chun school. She looked at her hands, still raw and stinging from her fall that morning. Hard as she tried, she couldn't stop thinking about the incident on the bleachers. The way the steps had seemed to disappear, leaving a gaping, dark hole full of hissing snakes. What had made her imagine such a thing?

Cassidy shifted her heavy backpack from her sore right shoulder to her left. She heard the jingling of the coins inside their wooden box.

Maybe Master Lau will know what the coins are, she thought. He had once told his class, *The student stands in a dark room while the master stands in the sunlight.* Well, she decided, as she thought about the strange gift of five coins that might not even be meant for her, she certainly felt as if she were standing in a dark room.

 Chapter Three

The bus jerked to a stop at the corner of South King Street. Cassidy saw Luis and Majesta leaning against the red brick wall along the front of Master Lau's studio. *Good, I'm early,* she thought. There was nothing worse than arriving late to Master Lau's class. If you were late, you were expected to make a formal apology, first to Master Lau, whom they addressed as "*Shifu*"—which meant "teacher and father"—and then to the other students. The apology had to be sincere and humble or you had to do it all over again. Master Lau would not accept a mumbling, eyes-down "I'm sorry." He would wait until he heard what he called *the true ring of apology* in the voice of the person who was unfortunate enough to arrive late for class. Cassidy had been late only two times in two years, and that was more than enough humiliation for her.

"Hey, Cass," Luis called to her. "Want to be my sticking-hands partner again today?" Luis Alvarez pushed up his baseball cap, and his dark eyes flashed at Cassidy. Black waves of hair spilled out from under his Seahawks cap. He held up both hands, palms toward Cassidy, as he did a quick circling move around her.

"Yeah, Luis, right," Cassidy said. "Don't expect to get so lucky two weeks in a row." Cassidy and Luis had been friends since sixth grade, when Luis transferred to Cleary Street Middle. He had also started Wing Chun classes just before Cassidy; they were practically at the same level. He circled her now, laughing and teasing. "Come on, Cassidy, put down your backpack and fight."

"Why don't you two grow up already?" Majesta said.

Majesta Madison was tall, thin, and drop-dead gorgeous. No matter how good Cassidy might be feeling about herself, if she spent much time in the cool circle of perfection that seemed to radiate from Majesta, she soon began to feel like a garden gnome.

"Come on, Majesta, why do you have to act like you're so much better than we are? You're only a year older than us," Luis pointed out.

"An *important* year older, though. I'm at Wilder High now," she said. "I'm a Wilder High *Panther*."

Luis turned his back to Majesta and rolled his eyes so that only Cassidy could see. A girl with dark wavy hair, wearing a pair of low-slung jeans and a creamy yellow fitted leather jacket, ran up to the building in a panic.

"It hasn't started?" she asked. "Thank God, I thought I was going to be late!" She bent at the waist and took a few deep breaths before looking over at Majesta. "Hey, girl, congratulations on making the squad! We're going to have a great time!"

"Thanks, Brooke, I couldn't believe it when they called my name!" Majesta said. "So are you in Master Lau's class?"

"Yeah," Brooke said. "My old teacher moved, and I heard that Master Lau's really good."

"He's a great teacher," Majesta said. "But completely and totally intimidating."

"You're right, though," Luis said. "He is the best."

"Yeah, that's why we're here," said Cassidy.

☙☙☙☙☙

As the students positioned themselves around the room, Luis leaned in to Cassidy and whispered,

"What do you think about the new bubble-head?"

"Don't know." Cassidy shrugged. "I'm guessing she's a cheerleader with Majesta at Wilder."

"I hate cheerleaders," Luis said in disgust. *"Yay, team! Go, team! Look at me, team!"*

"What have you got against cheerleaders, Luis?" Cassidy asked him, keeping her eye on the door to Master Lau's back office. Once the *shifu* stepped onto the training floor, all small talk was expected to stop immediately. "You have to be in really good shape to be a cheerleader—athletic, you know? That's probably why she's taking Wing Chun."

"Maybe," Luis replied. "I guess I like girls a little more brainy, like you, Cass. I haven't seen too many brainy cheerleaders."

Before Cassidy had a chance to respond, the door to Master Lau's office swung open and he stepped into the room. His gray hair was clipped short and emphasized his broad forehead and dark, serious eyes. His hands were clasped behind him as he walked silently across the floor and stood, unsmiling, in front of the class. The chatter stopped immediately as the twelve students stood in proper form and bowed, showing respect to their teacher, and then to each other.

Master Lau's class started with a warm-up. The students began jumping in one spot and then moved from side to side, then forward and back.

"Breathe correctly," Master Lau instructed them with a voice as crisp and dry as dead leaves. "Control your breath and you harness its power." Cassidy noticed Majesta on the other side of the room. Didn't the girl even sweat? At most she glowed, Cassidy thought with disgust. *Focus on what YOU can do*, Cassidy told herself. *Forget about Majesta.*

The students spent the next half hour doing paired kneeing and kicking drills followed by elbowing and punching. Cassidy smiled when she saw that Luis was paired with Brooke. He held the strike pad in place but unfortunately missed one of Brooke's cheerleader kicks, which made contact with his left shin. "Sorry, sorry, sorry," she heard Brooke murmur.

"Flow like water," Master Lau told them as he walked around the room, observing their drills. "Flow with the energy of your strike."

The *shifu* stopped in front of Luis and Brooke just at the moment that Brooke delivered a second kick toward the large square pad that Luis held in place. Her kick hit the pad with such force that Luis toppled backward. Red-faced for the second time in one day, Luis scrambled to his feet.

"Luis, please tell the class why you fell," Master Lau said. The class stopped their drills, waiting for the *shifu* to make a lesson out of Luis's fall.

"I wasn't prepared for the kick," Luis said, swallowing hard. Cassidy noticed that it was more of a question than a statement. Master Lau noticed it, too.

"Did you see Brooke as she raised her leg into kick position?" he asked.

"Yes, *Shifu*," Luis answered, his voice sounding thin and uncertain. Everyone dreaded being singled out this way by Master Lau, and Cassidy felt bad for her friend.

"Then why weren't you prepared? Think, Luis, there is a lesson here," Master Lau told him.

"I guess I wasn't expecting her kick to be so forceful," Luis said. Cassidy could tell by the way Luis answered that he hoped this was what Master Lau was looking for.

"Ah, you expected a light kick and you received a hard kick," said Master Lau. "I'm curious. Why would you expect a light kick?"

While Luis thought about the question, Cassidy glanced at Brooke, who looked as if she might cry. As if she was afraid she might be in trouble for knocking Luis to the ground.

"I wasn't expecting the kick to be so forceful because her other kicks and punches weren't very strong," Luis answered.

"Here is a lesson that came from my master and I give you today: *A battle is never won by underestimating the enemy.*"

"I understand, *Shifu*," Luis said, looking visibly relieved that the lesson was almost over.

"Now, students, there's something else to be

learned here as well. Before one can fight, one must learn to stand," said Master Lau, addressing his class. "We have been working on our animal forms. Today we will learn the crane stance."

Cassidy and the other students moved into a large circle with Master Lau at the center. Luis placed himself next to Cassidy and whispered, "I think I may have underestimated the cheerleader."

"You think?" Cassidy asked.

"The crane," Master Lau began, "is a graceful and patient animal. In ancient writings the crane is said to be deep in thought when in this position."

Master Lau stood with one foot planted firmly on the floor while his opposite knee was lifted, his upper thigh parallel to the ground, his arms outstretched. He stood for what seemed like forever, Cassidy thought, balanced perfectly on one leg, his face betraying no struggle to keep from falling over. As the students watched in silence, Cassidy wondered about Master Lau's age. He was certainly older than her father by a number of years, yet he didn't seem old at all. The strength and speed he demonstrated in class amazed his students.

"The crane stance is used to train inner balance," Master Lau told them. "When one has mastered inner balance, one is not so easily tipped over." Master Lau looked at Luis as he said this.

"Now, let's practice the stance of the crane," said Master Lau.

Cassidy lifted her right knee and positioned her left foot as Master Lau had demonstrated. The first attempt was a little shaky, and she was forced to bring her right foot back to the floor. *Balance,* she thought. *Take a deep breath and find your inner balance.* Cassidy visualized a white crane standing gracefully and patiently at the water's edge. She brought her right knee up again and stood firmly with her left foot on the floor.

Around her, Cassidy saw students attempting the difficult position and then failing. *I can't believe it,* she thought. *I'm actually good at this!*

Master Lau made his way over to Cassidy and stood at her side, observing her form. "Excellent balance," he said, then spoke to the rest of the class. "Notice, students, when the crane stance is done properly, one could balance a teacup on the knee without spilling a drop." Cassidy was beyond thrilled. Master Lau rarely used her as an example for the class, especially as an example of doing something well.

"Notice the placement of Cassidy's hands, palms up," Master Lau said as he circled her. "Her posture is straight . . ." he continued, lightly touching the top of her shoulder. At his touch Cassidy immediately lost her balance, bringing her right foot down hard.

"Sorry," she mumbled, embarrassed.

"You have nothing to be sorry about," Master Lau said. "The crane stance is quite difficult, but very important."

Cassidy rubbed her shoulder. Master Lau had barely touched her, but it had sent a spasm of pain through her arm.

"I'm sure that each of you will practice the crane this week," Master Lau said as he walked toward the front of the studio and prepared to dismiss class. The students bowed, saying, "Thank you, *Shifu*." Master Lau returned the bow and then raised his hand as a signal that class was over.

"You need a ride, Cass?" Luis asked. "My dad's picking me up today."

"Thanks anyway, Luis," Cassidy said. "I'm taking the bus." She needed to show the gold coins to Master Lau, and somehow she didn't want Luis or anyone else here to know about her strange birthday gift.

"Is it because I let that cheerleader knock me down? Is that why you've lost respect for me?"

"Well, a little . . ." Cassidy said, grinning. "Aw, I'm just kidding," she said, giving him a friendly swipe. "I'm actually really impressed by a guy who can get knocked on his butt by a cheerleader and isn't afraid to talk about it. It shows that you're in touch with your sensitive side."

Luis chuckled. "Sure you don't need a ride, Cass? I can wait."

"No, that's okay," Cassidy said. "I'm actually

meeting my parents for dinner, and it's in the opposite direction of where you're going."

"Okay, well, have a good time," said Luis as he headed for the door. "And don't worry about little ol' me and my sensitivity issue," he added, turning around. "We won't take it personally."

Master Lau's studio was housed in an old school gymnasium, and with the students gone, the large room seemed full of hollow echoes and deep pockets of shadows. Cassidy saw that the door to Master Lau's office was closed, but a sliver of light spilled out underneath.

As she made her way across the floor, Cassidy's shoes squeaked on the highly polished wood. Some movement near the far end of the gym caught her attention. Something flew past the light and disappeared behind a stack of benches. *It must be a bird,* Cassidy thought. *It probably got in through the window.* As she squinted to get a better look, she felt a dull pain behind her eyes and the beginning of a headache.

Maybe I need glasses, Cassidy thought. *Maybe that's why the steps blurred and I tripped today.* She noticed no other movement in the inky shadows of the old gymnasium and finally decided that her eyes were just playing tricks on her. Walking toward Master Lau's office, Cassidy thought she heard the fluttering sound of wings, but when she turned to look, she saw nothing out of the ordinary.

She glanced back toward the outside door, suddenly wishing she'd asked Luis to wait for her. She felt tired and dreaded the long bus ride home alone. Even more, she realized that she dreaded facing Master Lau. In the entire two years she'd taken lessons from him, she'd never been in his office.

You're being silly, she told herself. Why was she so afraid of talking to Master Lau? He was tough and mostly serious all the time, but he was also a great teacher whose classes were the high point of her week.

"Knowledge is power," she said under her breath before knocking on the door to Master Lau's office.

✿ Chapter Four

"*Shifu*, may I ask you a question?" she said, using the proper form he had taught them.

Master Lau was sitting at his desk with a ledger in front of him. "Of course, please, Cassidy, have a seat." He pointed to a straight wooden chair in front of his desk.

Cassidy sat down, reached into her backpack, and pulled out the carved box. She removed the top and shook the coins into her hand. "Can you tell me anything about these? Do you know what they are?" She opened her fingers to show him the coins in her hand, wondering if he noticed the red scraped flesh on her palm.

"Ah, let's see what you have," Master Lau said. He moved around to the front of his desk and pushed the ledger and some other books aside. "Place the coins here on the desk and let me take a closer look." He reached into a drawer and brought out a small magnifying glass. "My eyes aren't as sharp as they used to be," he explained.

Master Lau studied the coins. "What's on the other side?" he asked.

"Actually, nothing at all," Cassidy told him. One by one, she turned each coin over to show Master Lau the blank side.

"Well, they're not anything I recognize," he said at last. "They don't seem to be any type of coin or even personal seals that I'm aware of. Do you mind telling me where these came from?"

"They were a gift," Cassidy said. For a moment Cassidy thought of telling Master Lau about the stranger who gave her the box this morning, but she stopped.

"Quite an unusual gift, Cassidy," he said.

The *shifu* studied her face for a moment and seemed to be waiting for her to speak. She remembered that he once told his students, *When facing an opponent or a friend, it is in the pause when most is said.* Was he waiting for her to say more? Did he think that if he waited long enough, she would tell him where she got the coins?

"Thanks for looking at them, Master Lau, but I should probably go," Cassidy said at last. "My mom made me promise not to be late."

"If you like, you can leave the coins with me," Master Lau offered. "I'd be happy to do some research for you." He waved a hand toward a low shelf underneath the window, which was filled with books in Chinese. "They're certainly unusual. I'm sure you must be very curious."

"Yes, Master Lau, I am," Cassidy said. "Maybe I'll take them to the library or something. I'll let you know if I find out anything."

Cassidy gathered the coins and put them back in the box, sliding the top over the bottom. She stood up to leave. "Thanks again," she said. "See you next week."

"Certainly, Cassidy, next week," he said, bending to pick up something from the floor. Cassidy saw that he was holding the rice paper note with the name *Mingmei*. It must have fallen out of the box when she put the coins inside.

He held the paper out to her. "Have a happy birthday, Mingmei," he said.

Cassidy was startled to hear him say Mingmei. He must have assumed it was her Chinese name, and for all Cassidy knew, maybe it was. She mumbled a quick thank-you and walked out of the dim light of Master Lau's office into the eerie emptiness of the gymnasium.

She peered into the shadows but saw nothing fluttering. *Did the bird find its way out the window?* she wondered. *Or was there even a bird at all?* She pushed open the heavy door, which screeched on its hinges and echoed in the dusty shadows behind her. Shifting her backpack from one aching shoulder to the other, she walked out into the gray evening of Seattle at dusk.

ଈଈଈଈଈ

After Cassidy and her parents finished ordering dinner, Cassidy's dad proposed a birthday toast. "To our wonderful daughter, Cassidy, on her fourteenth birthday. We are so proud of you!"

They clinked glasses, and then Cassidy surprised them all by saying, "So, do you guys know anyone named Mingmei with the same birthday as mine?" It wasn't exactly how she'd planned to tell them about the coins, but hearing her name mentioned during the toast made her think about the way Master Lau had called her Mingmei earlier.

"Mingmei?" her father said. "Where did you hear that name?"

Cassidy placed the carved box on the table and

lifted the top. She showed her parents the note and the coins and told them the story about the man who had given them to her that morning.

"I don't like it," her mother said, her voice tight. "Who could it have been, Simon?"

Simon Chen turned the coins over and over in his hands as if an answer might appear on them at any moment.

"Describe him again, Cassidy," her father said. "Don't leave out a thing."

"He was an older Chinese man, maybe as old as Mrs. King next door. He had gray hair, kind of pushed back in the front. He had a nice face, I guess. I mean, it kind of surprised me when he just sort of appeared out of nowhere, so I'm not sure I really got a good look at his face. I think he was wearing a white shirt or jacket and maybe dark-colored pants. He was kind of short or, you know, average. That's all I remember. He just handed me the package, and then he was gone."

"He didn't speak?" Cassidy's dad asked.

"No, he didn't say anything. He probably thought I was someone named Mingmei."

"Too strange," her mother said. She was looking closely at each coin.

"Extremely strange," her father said. "Mingmei was the name your grandmother wanted you to have."

"She wanted you to name me Mingmei?

Why?"

"She said it was a good strong name—it means 'beautiful' and 'clever,'" Simon told her. "I guess I've always considered Mingmei to be your Chinese name."

"Actually," her mother said, "the name Cassidy means practically the same thing."

"That's weird," Cassidy said. "I've had this sort of other name all this time and I didn't even know it until today."

"No, what's weird is that a *stranger* showed up at the house and gave you a gift today," Wendy Chen said. "We need to know what's going on."

"Is there anything else you remember about him?" her father asked.

"Not really," Cassidy said. "He was just there and then he sort of disappeared."

"Disappeared? Cassidy, people don't just disappear," her father said.

"Oh, Dad, I don't mean actually *disappeared*. It was really foggy, and I guess he just walked away after he gave me the package and I couldn't see him anymore."

"What do you think this is about, Simon?" her mother asked. "Who would even know about Cassidy's other name?"

"Seriously, because *I* didn't even know about it," Cassidy said.

"That's the thing," Simon told them. "Your grandmother died right before you were born. There's nobody else—nobody who would know you as Mingmei."

"But *somebody* must know," her mother insisted. "Because *somebody* gave Cassidy this gift today with the name Mingmei on it."

"That's right, so the question is, *who*?" Cassidy said. She was trying to be logical about this, trying to ignore the tremor of fear that was moving through her.

Her father shook his head and looked across the room at the server coming to their table with a tray of food. "I really don't like this, Cassidy. Promise me not to talk to that man or engage him in any way if you see him again. And tell us immediately so that we can call the police. Promise?"

"I promise," said Cassidy.

"And now for gifts," Cassidy's mother said after the last bite of chocolate birthday cake and coconut ice cream.

Cassidy opened a neon green gift bag and found a tangerine wrap sweater that she'd admired at Loops last week. "Thanks, Mom, you remembered!" Cassidy said, and gave her mother a hug.

"And here's a little one," her dad said as he handed her a small package wrapped in pale pink and tied with a silver ribbon.

Cassidy knew that inside she would find a charm. For birthdays and all major gift-giving holidays, she received a charm for the sterling silver bracelet her parents had given her when she was five. Her parents understood that she felt too grown-up to actually wear the charm bracelet, but they continued giving her charms anyway, saying that one day she would look back at the charms on the bracelet and have a special memory connected with each one. Cassidy now had everything from a sterling silver tooth that signified the first tooth she lost in kindergarten to a small yellow enamel cat to mark the day they adopted Monty from the animal shelter.

She slipped the pink paper from the box and held up the new charm. It was a small dog carved in jade.

"Does this mean I'm getting a dog?" Cassidy asked excitedly.

"Ah, no, not exactly," her dad said. "This little dog is actually a good luck charm—for good luck in your fourteenth year!"

"They didn't have a four-leaf clover?" Wendy asked.

"That's too common. I wanted this to be special. I guess it's kind of a connection to your Chinese heritage, Cassidy," her dad explained. "This carving is based on a statue of a temple guardian that was found in China. I chose it because you were born in the Year of the Dog. Traditional Chinese horoscopes say that makes you smart, brave, and loyal. All true."

"That's sweet, Dad, I love it," Cassidy told him. "I could have used a guardian charm this morning. I tripped like a complete klutz on the steps in the gym." She held out both scraped palms. A pale, purplish bruise had formed on her left hand and spread up into the delicate blue veins of her wrist. Cassidy decided not to mention the weird way the steps had seemed to disappear, causing her to fall. Her mother would have her scheduled the next day for everything from eye exams to brain scans.

"Ouch," Wendy said. "Let's get some ointment on that when we get home."

"It doesn't hurt so much now," Cassidy said. "It was mostly just embarrassing." But she realized that it did hurt. In fact, not only did her palms still sting, but both arms felt heavy and ached with a dull pain.

"Thank you both for the gifts," she said. "I absolutely love the sweater, Mom. And Dad, the charm is the best ever." She held the small green dog in her bruised, stinging hand and wondered about what kind of luck she might need in her fourteenth year.

🌸 Chapter Five

All was dark, and then an opening appeared and behind the opening, an eye. The eye blinked once, then twice. On the third blink a beautiful woman stood at the foot of Cassidy's bed. She was dressed in a traditional Chinese high-necked silk tunic and trousers, both of a smoky tangerine color. She opened her arms, and a soft light filled the room. The woman smiled and said, "Daughter of Light." Cassidy sat up in bed.

"We have been waiting for this day." Another woman, dressed in a similar tunic and trousers in apricot silk, appeared next to the first, and they greeted each other with an embrace as each said, "Sister!"

"As it was told over three hundred years ago, so it has come to pass. You have been chosen, Mingmei. A princess! The first girl born of our crossed bloodlines! Much has been given to you!" said the first woman.

"And much is expected from you," said the second.

Cassidy listened but was unable to speak.

"Five evil spirits have been awakened. These are the spirits of old enemies that we defeated in the mountains," explained the first woman.

"These spirits are restless now and want revenge, Mingmei," said the second woman. "As you are of our blood, they will try to destroy you."

At last Cassidy found her voice. "Destroy me? What am I supposed to do?"

"You must defeat each of the five spirits in order to fulfill your destiny! You can't run any longer."

"I don't understand," said Cassidy.

"You will understand," said the first woman as she smiled. "You have been given a gift, and you will receive more."

The images of the women began to fade.

"Don't go!" Cassidy pleaded. "What if I don't want to do this?"

"You're a warrior now—a warrior princess. You cannot run from or change this destiny," said the first woman. "It has already begun!"

As Cassidy struggled to see the fading images of the

two figures, the second woman held out a hand, and Cassidy saw that it contained a white feather. "Being a warrior is a lonely fate," said the woman. "But an ally will find you. Be careful of whom you trust."

𖤐 𖤐 𖤐 𖤐 𖤐

Cassidy was awoken by a heavy thud on her chest. It was Monty, and he appeared very agitated. He refused to relax in her arms the way he normally did. "What's wrong, kitty?" Cassidy asked.

Monty jumped to the floor of the darkened bedroom. Cassidy glanced at her alarm clock — it was 4 A.M. — and switched on her bedside lamp.

As the light filled the room, she remembered her dream. Two women. *They called me Mingmei. Evil spirits that I must destroy. What a strange dream*, Cassidy thought. While Monty paced the floor and made small growling sounds deep in his chest, Cassidy wrote down everything she could remember about the dream.

She remembered that one of the women said, "You can't run any longer." *Weird*, she thought, *but good if it means I won't have any more running dreams*. The running dreams always left her feeling drained and exhausted.

Cassidy tried to let other memories come to her. She remembered the women calling her *Daughter of Light* and a *warrior princess*. And explaining that five spirits wanted revenge and that Cassidy must destroy them.

There was something else. Cassidy tried to remember the last thing the woman said before fading away. Oh yeah: *An ally will find you. Be careful of whom you trust.*

As she scribbled the words into her dream journal, Monty jumped onto her lap, causing her pen to scratch a thin blue line across the paper. "Yeah, you're some ally," she said to him. The yellow cat pushed his head against Cassidy's hand, as if he wanted her to stop writing and hold him.

"Okay, okay, I get the message," she said. She put the journal away and turned out her light, hoping to get a few hours of sleep before her alarm went off. Monty curled next to her but then sprang up again, too restless to sleep.

"Come on, you crazy cat," she told him, yawning. "Settle down."

As she drifted off to sleep, she was somewhat aware that Monty continued to pace the floor at the foot of her bed, occasionally leaping at shadows.

᧍᧍᧍᧍᧍

After a quick shower later that morning, Cassidy walked into her bedroom, pulling her damp hair into a ponytail. In a blurry flash of yellow-orange fur,

Monty leaped from the foot of the bed to the dresser. He pawed at the carved box of coins that Cassidy had taken out of her backpack the night before.

"No, Monty," she said. But before she could reach him, he had swatted the box to the floor, the coins inside jingling against one another. Monty jumped down after his "prey," sniffing at the corner of the box.

"Sorry, Monty. It's not yours," Cassidy said. She picked up the box and slipped it into a drawer on top of a stack of folded T-shirts. "It's only yours if your name's Mingmei," she told him.

"All aboard," Cassidy's mom called from below. "The Chen train's pulling out in two minutes!"

"Coming, Mom," Cassidy answered. She grabbed a homework printout and stuffed it into her backpack. "See ya, you kooky cat," she said.

Monty sat as still as a sphinx, staring at Cassidy's dresser drawer.

ⓔⓔⓔⓔⓔ

Cassidy was trying to reach a book that was wedged into the far corner of her locker when Eliza walked up. "Oh my God, Eliza, what did you do to your hair?" Cassidy asked.

"You like?" Eliza turned around and shook her hair from side to side. There were several blue and orange stripes interspersed with Eliza's natural honey blond hair. "School colors. I think this shows just how much school spirit I have for cheerleader tryouts, don't you?"

Cassidy touched a bluish lock of hair that fell across Eliza's forehead and laughed. "I think it definitely shows that you have school spirit."

"Is it too much?" Eliza asked nervously. "A committee of teachers and other adults makes the final decision about who gets on the squad. You think they'll get what I'm doing, understand what kind of statement it makes?"

"Of course," Cassidy told her. "They'd be crazy not to get it."

"Seriously?" Eliza asked. "Come on, Cass, I really, *really* want to be a cheerleader."

"I'm positive they'll understand your . . . your statement."

"I had a dream the other night," Eliza said. "In my dream, there was this big game and the stands were full of people. I was out there cheering and my hair was like this. I figured it's a sign. I told Mom about it and she said, 'Let's do it.' It'll wash out, so it's really no big deal."

Cassidy thought about some of the dreams she'd had. *It's a good thing I don't take my dreams so literally,* she thought. *Otherwise I'd be fighting some demon because two women told me I had to.*

As they walked to class, Cassidy told Eliza about the dream of the two women who appeared in her room.

"I totally know what that means," Eliza said, stopping right in the middle of the hall. "I can't believe you haven't figured it out already."

"That I'm going to get in some kind of fight this year?" Cassidy asked. "I could so get kicked out of school for that, Eliza."

"No, I'm serious, Cass. Think about it," Eliza said, looking as if she couldn't believe that Cassidy couldn't see the obvious. "It means that you should try out for cheerleader, too! Think about it—who are we? Hello? The Cleary Street *Warriors*!"

"I already told you, Eliza, I'm busy with Wing Chun and . . . I don't know. I don't think I'm the cheerleader type."

"But come on, the *dream*," Eliza continued. "You'll win a spot on the cheerleading squad—the *Warriors* squad—and then other girls will be mad because you made it and they didn't. They'll want revenge. And what else did you say about an ally? An ally will find you? Exactly! Me—it means that I'll be your ally on the squad!"

"That's pretty good, Eliza. You ought to charge for this dream interpretation thing you do."

Eliza sniffed and looked away. "It's a gift," she said. "It wouldn't be right to profit from it, but all donations are gratefully accepted."

"We'd better get to class," Cassidy said as the bell rang. "Only a few more periods to go."

"And then it's time for tryouts!" Eliza said as she practically sprinted down the hall, her blue-and-orange hair flying behind her. She stopped and looked back at Cassidy. "You really, *really* need to think about this—I think your dream is telling you to try out, like you're *destined* to be a cheerleader or something!"

Cassidy thought about Eliza's interpretation of her dream as she glanced over at the school emblem above the trophy case. A large, fierce-looking eagle held several arrows in his right claw. Cassidy pictured the Cleary Street Warriors team—a bunch of eighth-grade boys running around in muddy football uniforms—and shook her head.

She didn't have a clue what her dream really meant. But somehow she didn't think it had anything to do with being a middle school cheerleader.

❧❧❧❧❧

As Cassidy headed toward her last class of the day, she caught a glimpse of something flying through the air at the far end of the corridor. The orange-and-blue Cleary banner that hung on the wall by the office swung slightly as if it were being disturbed by something behind it. Did anyone else see it? She looked around and then back toward the shiny satin banner, but this time it was perfectly still.

"Yo, Cassidy." Luis bumped against her shoulder. "Wanna go to the sci-fi festival at Wall Splash? It's all eighties flicks."

Wall Splash showed movies on the outside wall of a warehouse. People brought their own chairs—even sofas—and watched under the stars. "Maybe," she said distractedly. "Luis, did you see anything fly behind that banner—down by the office?" Cassidy nodded toward the far end of the hall.

"Fly?" Luis asked, and looked toward the banner. "You mean a bird or something?"

"I guess it's nothing," Cassidy said. "Must have been the way the light hit it." A sharp pulsing began behind Cassidy's eyes, and she squinted and rubbed her temples.

"You seeing things, Cass?" Luis asked, grinning. "Hearing things, too? Little voices in your head?"

"Never mind," Cassidy said. "I'm going to get some water. Catch you later."

"Later," Luis said. "Call me if you want to go to that festival."

"Okay." Cassidy walked to a nearby water fountain and leaned over for a drink. The headache that began behind her eyes spread into an intense tightening at her forehead so that it felt as if a metal band were wrapped around her head. Her ears rang with the pain, and she stood for a moment with her back against the wall, realizing that her vision had blurred into a tiny pinpoint of light. She took another long drink of water and several deep breaths until the feeling began to pass.

Okay, she told herself, *you've got one more class. You'll feel better once you sit down.* But as she started down the hall, Cassidy's eyes were again drawn to the orange-and-blue banner that hung beside the office. She stopped and watched it as it fluttered unnaturally.

Chapter Six

By the time the last bell rang, Cassidy was more than ready to leave school and head down the sidewalk toward her mom's preschool. She helped out at the Happy Bunny whenever she could.

As she passed the marshy edge of the lake, she noticed a crane standing perfectly still and balanced on one leg. Cassidy stepped off the sidewalk and walked down the slatted boardwalk path to see it better. She wondered if Master Lau was right and the crane was thinking deep thoughts.

"I can do it, too," she told the uninterested bird.

Cassidy assumed the crane stance. "See," she said. Then, in a sudden white flurry of angled wings and large body, the crane took off, beating its wings once, then twice, gaining altitude before gliding across the lake and out of sight.

"Hmmm, jealous?" Cassidy asked. She looked down and saw that the crane had left behind several white feathers. She picked one up and slipped it into her backpack.

❧❧❧❧❧

When she got home that afternoon, Cassidy found a message from Eliza with the good news that she'd made the cheerleading squad. Cassidy called her back. "Want to come for a sleepover tomorrow night? Mom and Dad want to make dinner to honor you for making cheerleader."

"That's sweet!" Eliza said. "Your mom and dad are so cool, Cassidy."

"I guess," Cassidy said. "I mean, yeah, they're pretty great. Anyway, can you come? Dad said he'll make veggie lasagna."

"I'm there!" Eliza said. "That's my favorite!"

❧❧❧❧❧

At dinner on Friday night, Eliza told the Chens

about her new diet. "I call it 'Eating Up to the Line,'" she explained. With the edge of her fork, she drew a line across the cheesy top of her serving of lasagna. "Now, what I do is just eat *up* to the line. I never go over the line. That way I get to eat all the foods I like, but just not as much."

"Interesting, Eliza," Simon Chen said. "And you came up with this on your own?"

"Yeah, I really think it's a great idea, too. Maybe I should write a book — *Eliza's Eating Up to the Line Diet*. I can totally see Oprah reading it and then having me on her show."

"Very clever, Eliza," said Cassidy's mother. "I'm wondering, though, do you really think you need to lose weight? I'm sure you get quite a workout practicing all those cheers."

"Yeah, well, I can't rely on burning calories alone. You should see some of the size zeros on the squad! I'll look like a cow next to them — major bovine!"

"Nobody's a cow," said Simon the peacemaker. "Now, let's eat our lasagna and change the subject."

"Just up to the line," muttered Eliza.

৩৩৩৩৩

The next morning the girls were woken up by Monty when he jumped on the bed and began kneading

Eliza's blue-and-orange hair.

"Weird," Eliza told Cassidy as she sat up in bed. "I was dreaming that somebody was washing my hair, and then I wake up to find Monty with his paws all over my head. I'll have to put that in my dream journal. Do you still write down your dreams?"

"Yeah, sure," Cassidy told her.

"Me too," Eliza said. "I had a really freaky dream a couple of nights ago—I got home from school, and there was a moving van at the apartment. Mom had already loaded everything."

"She's not talking about moving again, is she?" Cassidy asked.

"Just every time she has a bad day!"

There was a knock at the door, and Wendy Chen poked her head in. "I thought I heard some morning chatter," she said. "I'm going to Pike Place Market this morning, so if you two want to come with, better get up and at 'em!"

"Great," said Cassidy. "Yeah, we want to go— just give us a chance to get ready."

"There's cereal and milk downstairs," her mom said. "Although I really don't know how Eliza will manage eating up to the line on a bowl of cereal."

"Ha, very funny," Eliza said, picking up her overnight bag and heading into the bathroom to get ready.

Cassidy reached into her dresser to pull out a

clean T-shirt. There was the box of coins the strange old man had given her on her birthday. It still didn't make any sense. She hadn't seen him again, but her mom and dad asked her about him almost every day. Her dad had even called some distant relatives in China and asked them if they knew anybody who might have known about the name Mingmei. But her dad's cousin knew nothing, and his elderly uncle had had a stroke several years before and couldn't speak.

She shook the coins into her hands and noticed again the scraped flesh on her palms. The bruise that had formed along her wrist had now spread to her forearm and was a sickly greenish yellow.

Eliza came back into the room wearing emerald green cords and an oversized pink sweater that ended in black-and-white fringe that hung almost to her knees.

"Have you found out any more about the coins?" Eliza asked, retying a length of loose fringe.

"Not really. Maybe I'll Google them later and see what's there," Cassidy said. "About all I've figured out is they can't be real gold. Who would give gold coins to a perfect stranger?"

"You never know," Eliza said airily. "But if they are gold, I've got one word for you: eBay. My mom's started to make a real killing selling all the retro and vintage stuff she's been buying up."

Later that morning, when Wendy drove over to Sally Mander's to pick up some books for the Happy Bunny, she dropped Cassidy and Eliza off on the same shopping street so they could do some shopping of their own. At least that's what Cassidy and Eliza told her they'd be up to. Instead they planned to visit an antique store Eliza knew about from her mom's new eBay project. "There it is," Eliza said, nodding toward a dark, narrow storefront tucked in between the Go-Go, the vintage clothing store, and the Bay North Art Gallery. "This is so exciting. What if they're worth a ton of money?"

"I doubt an absolute stranger would have given them up if they're worth that much," Cassidy said.

"Only one way to find out," Eliza said.

 Chapter Seven

The name of the shop was written in small red letters on the door: *The Chinese Tiger Antiques and Gifts.* As Eliza waited outside, Cassidy went in. Bare bulbs hung from long cords and scattered weak yellow pools of light around the store, illuminating stone pots, porcelain bowls, and small rosewood and black lacquer tables. Silk and paper scrolls hung on one wall.

A Chinese man reading a newspaper sat at a massive desk painted moss green. Yellow and orange birds were painted around the lower edge of the desk, and above the birds were lotus blossoms. The design looked as if it might have been bright at one time, but years, maybe even centuries, had aged it to subtle, more muted shades.

The man peered at Cassidy over the top of his reading glasses. "Is there something I can help you with?" he asked as he put down the newspaper.

Cassidy realized she was the only customer. Outside, the bustle of a busy Saturday passed by the Chinese Tiger's narrow door, but inside, the store was as quiet as dust.

"I have some coins," she began, her voice sounding loud in the small shop. "I was wondering if you could tell me anything about them."

The man motioned for Cassidy to come closer. She opened the box and placed the coins on the burnished red leather blotter on top of the desk. Methodically he picked up each coin and rubbed the smooth side with his thumb. Taking a large magnifying glass from a drawer in the green desk, he closely examined the engraving on each coin. Cassidy noticed a trio of small wrinkles form between his eyebrows as he studied the coins.

"Don't know. I'm afraid I can't help you," he said finally, putting the coins down and pushing them away slightly. "But thank you for coming in."

"Are you saying you've never seen any coins like them before?" Cassidy asked, somewhat surprised at his abruptness.

"I'm saying I can't tell you *exactly* what they are. I've seen plenty of old coins, but none like these. These are . . ."

"They're what?" Cassidy asked, puzzled at his long pause and the odd, nervous way he was behaving.

"Well, they're very old, for one thing," he said. "They're also probably the only ones of their kind."

"Are they something you'd be interested in buying for your shop? I mean, if you've never seen any like them before, they must be kind of valuable, right?"

"Valuable, yes, I'm certain they're gold. But do I want these coins for my shop? Absolutely not. To be honest with you, I don't even like them on my desk. I wish you'd put them back in the box. I get a bad feeling about these coins."

"Bad feeling?" Cassidy asked. "They're just old coins."

"Bad chi." He shook his head. "I'm not interested."

"Bad chi?" she repeated.

"Life force, the natural flow. These coins seem very wrong. Like I said, bad chi."

"Do you know anybody, like a coin dealer or someone, who could tell me what they are?"

"No, nobody," he said. Cassidy noticed that the man seemed more and more nervous about having the coins on his desk. He glanced at them, an odd expression on his face, and then looked quickly away.

"What do you think I should do with them?" she asked as she began gathering the coins to put them back in the box.

"If they were mine," he said, lowering his voice, "I'd bury them in the deepest hole I could dig."

⌒⌒⌒⌒⌒

"So, what did you find out? Did you sell them?" Eliza asked. Cassidy was sitting on a bench in front of Sally Mander's, waiting for her mother.

"Nope, not exactly," she told Eliza. "He didn't want them."

"Did he at least tell you what they are?"

"Just that they're old. Oh yeah, he said they're probably valuable. Apparently they're real gold."

"But he wouldn't buy them? Didn't he even make you an offer?"

"He didn't like them," Cassidy said. "He didn't want them for his shop."

"Why not? He should at least tell us what they're worth. Then Mom can put them on eBay for you."

"No, forget it, Eliza," Cassidy said. "I don't think he'd even tell us, anyway. He said he got a bad feeling from them. He was nervous about having them in his shop."

"Oh my God, Cassidy, that's seriously spooky! Are you saying the coins are—I don't know—*haunted* or something?"

"No, I'm not saying they're haunted! Do you hear how that sounds?" Cassidy asked. "What's that even mean—*they're haunted*? They're coins, Eliza, just old coins, that's all. The guy in the shop was probably just superstitious."

Eliza glanced into the bookshop window with a frown. "I see your mom up at the checkout. Maybe you should tell her about the haunted coins. I'm starting to get spooked."

"No," Cassidy said as her mother came out of Sally Mander's with two more huge shopping bags. "And the coins are not *haunted*! That sounds ridiculous and you know it."

"Ready to go, girls?" Wendy asked a few moments later. "Sorry, I didn't mean to keep you waiting so long."

"It's okay, Mom," Cassidy said, taking one of the bags of books. "We've just been . . . hanging out. It's fine."

ଚ୭ଚ୭ଚ୭ଚ୭ଚ୭

Once the threesome got to the car, Wendy reached into her shopping bags and pulled out a tiny cellophane sack filled with gold powder and passed it to Cassidy. It was marked *Fairy dust.*

"Isn't this cute?" Wendy asked. "They were selling these by the register. Reminded me of my grandmother Fiona. She believed in all kinds of magic—she even took me out in the forest once and showed me how to find 'real fairy dust.'"

"Real fairy dust?" Eliza asked. "What was it really?"

Wendy laughed and began loading the bags of books into the car. "Well, at the time, I really thought it was fairy dust. Actually, I'm not sure what it was—something that grew on a tree—little pods or blossoms or something. Anyway, she would pop them open and this yellow-gold dust burst out."

"Cool," Eliza said. "And you thought it was really magic?"

"Yeah, I did," Wendy said. "She'd sprinkle the yellow fairy dust on a pebble, or a bird's feather, or anything, really—and it became a good luck charm. She even sprinkled some on my head once and said that I'd be *forever lucky* and that it would be passed on to my children. So, Cassidy, I guess that makes you one of the *forever lucky* ones, too!"

But Cassidy wasn't feeling exactly lucky. And despite what she'd said to Eliza, she wasn't sure that the owner of the antique shop was just superstitious. She kept seeing the expression on his face in that moment before she'd returned the coins to their box. The man had been terrified.

❧ Chapter Eight

That evening Cassidy took the coins out of the box and laid them out on her bed. *Bad chi*, the antiques guy said, but here, in her familiar, cozy room, his reaction didn't seem nearly so spooky. *That's crazy*, she told herself. *They're just five old coins.*

She looked at each one closely the way the shopkeeper had, starting with the snake coin. She examined the side with the engraving to see if she'd missed anything before. Nope, the image of the coiled rope or serpent was exactly as she remembered it. She turned it over. The thick edge of the heavy coin was smooth, and the back was blank. *Wait a minute, it's not blank. There's something on the back.* She looked more closely. There was a small line that might be either horizontal or vertical depending on how you held the coin in your hand.

She checked the other four coins. They each had a different number of lines on the back, ranging from one line on the back of the snake coin to five lines on the back of the one with the openmouthed faces. Cassidy wondered whether the lines represented the value of the coins or possibly some type of ordering.

I think it's time for a little research, she told herself. She turned on her computer, and when the start-up chimes rang out, Monty came pouncing into the room.

"Hey, kitty cat, where've you been all afternoon?" She pulled him onto her lap while waiting for the web page to come up. Still holding him in her arms, she went over to the bed and scooped up the five coins in her right hand. As she sat back down at her desk, Monty sniffed at Cassidy's closed hand.

"You think this is a kitty treat?" she asked. Cassidy opened her right hand so Monty could see what she held. As if a wolf had sprung up from Cassidy's palm, Monty's fear reflex kicked in. The cat's claws shot out as he leaped away, leaving two bloody scratches on the inside of Cassidy's right arm.

"What's wrong with you?" she asked, rubbing

the stinging wounds. But Monty was already out the bedroom door, and as Cassidy went across the hall to the bathroom to clean her arm, she saw him race down the stairs, his tail fluffed out in fear.

Cassidy returned to her bedroom a few moments later, puzzled by what had happened. She picked up the coins that she'd dropped when Monty scratched her. *Weird cat! Does he sense some kind of bad chi like the guy at the Chinese Tiger? But that's silly,* she told herself. *There's some logical explanation for all of this. I just need to find out what the coins are, that's all.*

Cassidy began typing in search terms and found pages and pages of sites, but none of them sounded very relevant. She continued to scroll until she found a reference to an ancient Chinese custom in which warriors would celebrate a victory by having a gold coin made to mark the defeat of a particularly powerful enemy.

She picked up one of the coins and looked at it. Had this coin been made because some fighter, long ago, defeated a . . . *What is it—a rope? No, definitely not a rope; something else. It must be a snake.*

This business of trying to research mysterious gold coins was all a bit frustrating. It never seemed to reap any answers. Only more questions. Cassidy decided there would be time for more investigation later. She had some homework to do, and now was as good a time as any to start it.

As the students took their places in Wing Chun class the following week, Cassidy saw the door to Master Lau's office open. Expecting the *shifu* to step out, she was surprised instead to see an incredibly gorgeous, if slightly sullen-looking guy amble across the floor and take an empty spot near the side door. The expression on his face gave off the message that it would take a lot to impress him.

He had definite Chinese features and dark hair that was slightly long so that it fell at just the right sort of natural, who-cares angle across his forehead. He was tall and thin, but not too tall or too thin. He was, Cassidy thought as she watched him cross the floor, *perfect*. She didn't want to look away, but she knew how totally embarrassed she would be if he caught her staring at him.

"Hey," Majesta said to him, to which he nodded. Cassidy wondered if they were both at Wilder High. *He must be, like, sixteen at least.*

"When the mother ship returns you to Earth," Luis was saying, "I'd like you to answer my question."

"What?" Cassidy asked. "Sorry, Luis, I was just—"

Master Lau stepped out of his office, which

immediately ended all conversation.

Master Lau introduced the new student simply by saying, "We are joined today by James Tang. Please make him feel welcome."

The other students looked over at James, giving a little nod or a quiet *hey*. James gave his own slight nod to the other students. He looked not at all interested in being there with them.

Master Lau had the students begin by reviewing the crane stance. "We will see who devoted some time to practice this week," he said.

Once again Cassidy was able to expertly assume the stance. Luis was having difficulty, and so was Majesta. But James, Cassidy noticed, stood perfectly, effortlessly balanced.

Cassidy tried to focus her attention on Master Lau's instruction but again and again found herself looking over at James. It was apparent that he was good at everything—not just the crane stance. *Is that why he seems so bored?* Cassidy wondered. *Why is he in this class? Shouldn't he be in a more advanced Wing Chun? The way my luck is going, Master Lau will transfer him out after he sees how good he is at all the forms.*

"*Chi sau*—sticking hands," Master Lau announced, returning to the front of the room. He began pairing students for sticking hands, a close-range, hand-and-arm drill designed to help them develop a heightened sense of awareness of an opponent.

Master Lau nodded at Luis and then pointed to Cassidy. Luis happily walked over to Cassidy's side. Master Lau often paired Luis and Cassidy for sticking hands because they were at approximately the same level. Cassidy liked Luis but was starting to get the feeling that he was interested in being more than just a buddy.

"Move in close," Master Lau told the class. "Fingers to fingers, elbows to elbows—almost touching. No more than the thinnest of rice paper should be able to pass through the space between sticking hands."

"Not that close, Luis," Cassidy muttered under her breath, but Master Lau heard her.

"Yes, close!" he said, and he repositioned their forearms and pointed out to the other students how close the arms should be. "*Chi sau!* Feel your opponent's energy. Move with it. If you learn to sense the commitment in your opponent's wrist or elbow, then you will know his next move!"

Cassidy, following the *shifu's* instruction, ignored Luis's grin and concentrated on the drill. When Luis moved his arm, even a fraction, Cassidy was right there—moving with it and sensing his next move. She watched Luis's eyes and felt, rather than saw, what his intentions were. *This is wild,* she thought. *I may actually be getting better at Wing Chun than Luis!*

Near the end of class, Master Lau held up his right hand as a signal for everyone to stop their drills.

When all was quiet, he asked, "What is the ultimate aim of kung fu?" The students replied in unison, "Unity of mind, body, and spirit."

"That's correct," he replied. "One may use the body to demonstrate the correct forms and drills, but if the mind and spirit aren't involved, then the effort is hopelessly wasted." Cassidy didn't think it was her imagination that Master Lau looked directly at James Tang as he spoke.

Glancing at the new student, Cassidy realized that he didn't seem to notice that Master Lau's words were meant for him. James looked straight ahead, his dark eyes a complete mystery.

🌸 *Chapter Nine*

Cassidy arrived fifteen minutes early for Wing Chun class the following Wednesday. She stood outside against the wall and waited, wondering if James might show up early, too. She had admitted to Eliza that she had a crush on James, and Eliza had convinced her that talking to him was the only way to go. Maybe today was the day.

Unfortunately, when James appeared, he was walking side by side with none other than Majesta. *Did they come together?* Cassidy wondered.

"Hi," Cassidy said, looking at James. *He looks*

even better up close.

"Hey . . . you're the one with perfect crane form," James said, and gave her one of the most gorgeous smiles she had ever seen. *So he was watching. Does he really mean it? Or is he being sarcastic?*

"I wouldn't say perfect," Cassidy said.

Majesta was quick to interrupt. "So, James, how long did you say you've been in Seattle?"

"Since August, just in time to start the new year at Bainbridge High," he said. "I was born in Hong Kong, then moved to San Francisco. My dad got a job at the University of Washington, so we moved up here."

"U Dub," Cassidy and Majesta said in unison. When James looked confused, Majesta said, "It's what we call the University of Washington—U of W—U Dub."

"I'll try to remember that," James said.

"So you've been taking Wing Chun awhile?" Cassidy asked. "I mean, you pretty much have all the forms down."

"Yeah, too long," James said.

"We better go in," she said with a glance toward the door. "You don't want to know what happens if you're late to Master Lau's."

"Let me guess," he said. "The big apology, the asking-for-forgiveness bit, right?"

"Exactly," Majesta said. "Did your other

teachers do that, too?"

"Yeah, Lau's no different from the rest," he said.

"Ask yourself why you are here," began the *shifu*. Cassidy wondered what had prompted this lesson. Occasionally Master Lau liked to give them a few minutes of what he called the *philosophy of kung fu*. Usually he did this when he thought that the students weren't taking the classes seriously.

"The wisdom of kung fu," he continued, "can be applied to any situation you may find yourself in. Kung fu teaches you to be in control of yourself. One finds true strength and inner peace when mind, body, and spirit work as one. Conflict arises when this is not in balance."

Okay, I get it, Cassidy thought. *This is another lesson for the benefit of James Tang.* She stole a quick look his way. But just as before, if James was aware that he was the focus of Master Lau's lesson, he certainly didn't show it. And when the *shifu* ended the philosophy lesson, James once again demonstrated flawless drills, perfect form, and utter boredom.

At the end of class that day, Majesta, Luis, James, and Cassidy were the last ones to leave the studio. Luis, quiet for a change, crossed the street and walked toward the bus stop at the corner. Cassidy hung back on the sidewalk, hoping to learn a little more about James. *Why is he even here if he's so bored?* she wondered.

"How come you're not taking the more advanced classes?" Majesta asked him. "You're definitely good enough."

James shrugged. "They meet at night, and my dad thinks I should be home studying at night. I don't really want to have to work that hard, anyway."

"Then why are you here?"

"Because my dad thinks it's good for me," James replied. "And I want to keep my dad happy right now because I'd like my own car before I get too old to drive."

Cassidy found this totally intriguing. James was movie-star handsome, but there was something else, too. He had this sort of sullen, defiant look that seemed to say, *This is what I am. If you don't like it, too bad.*

Cassidy looked toward the cross-street half a block down and saw the bus turn the corner. "I've gotta go," she said. "Bus is coming."

"Yeah, me too, my sister's here," said Majesta, motioning toward a VW Bug that just pulled up to the curb. "You need a ride, James?"

"No, thanks anyway," James said, and then he turned to Cassidy. "See you later, Crane Girl."

Crane Girl? Is he flirting with me?

"My bus is here," she said, wishing she didn't have to leave at just the moment when James might or might not be flirting with her. "See you next week."

With her backpack slung over one shoulder, Cassidy took a quick glance down the street and then ran toward the waiting bus parked at the opposite curb. Halfway across, Cassidy heard an earsplitting shriek that stopped her in her tracks.

She looked up in horror to see the gaping chrome mouth of—of what? A large, dark bulk bore down on her, jaws gaped open, ready to eat her alive. *Not real, this is not real!* she tried to tell herself. But she knew what she was seeing with her own eyes, and she also knew that she was totally unable to move— to get away from it! She stared into the open mouth full of sharp, metallic teeth, the ripping, shredding kind of teeth designed to strip flesh from bones. She remembered a terrifying sea creature she'd seen at the aquarium once—a giant eel or something—with a long, thick body and rows of razor-edged teeth. The creature roared and shrieked in fury—its eyes blazed pure white-hot hate.

"What are you doing?" a man shouted. "Get out of the way!"

Cassidy blinked and looked toward the voice. A man in a chauffeur's cap leaned out the window of a long, dark stretch limo. "What's wrong with you!" he shouted again. "Move it!"

It's not a monster, Cassidy realized. *But . . . but it was a monster! I saw its mouth—its eyes—it shrieked! But had it? Maybe I just saw the chrome grill, the headlights. Maybe the shriek was really the squealing tires, the blaring horn. What's wrong with me?*

She felt frozen, unable to continue toward the bus or step back on the sidewalk.

"Are you okay?" James started toward her.

"I'm — I'm fine," she said, suddenly embarrassed. *I was almost killed, but I'm fine.* She waved James away, picked up her backpack, and ran toward the bus, which had just started to close its doors. Her heart raced. *What just happened? I'm sure I looked down the street before crossing! Nothing was there!*

She slid into the empty seat beside Luis. "Did you see that?" she asked him. "That limo—it almost hit me!"

"Yeah, you okay?" Luis asked. "What happened?"

"It just came out of nowhere," she told him, willing her heart to beat at a more normal pace. "And then it seemed like I couldn't move, like I was frozen right there in the middle of the street." *Can I tell Luis what I really saw? This is crazy!*

"Actually, Cass, I was looking out the window, and it kind of seemed like you just ran across the street in front of it. Didn't you see it?"

Did I see it? No, I didn't see anything at all, and then when I started across, there it was, and it looked like a monster eel—not a stretch limo.

"I looked," she told Luis. "But I guess I just didn't see it."

"It was kind of hard to miss, Cass," Luis said. "Maybe you just had something else on your mind. Or maybe *someone* else."

Cassidy looked at Luis. *Does he know how I feel about James?*

Luis shrugged and said, "Just a thought."

Yeah, just a thought, but maybe Luis is right. She replayed the last few minutes in her mind. *James flashed me this devastatingly white smile and called me Crane Girl. Then I ran across the street and almost got killed. Is it possible,* she wondered, *that a boy could smile at you once and you'd completely lose your mind?*

❧ Chapter Ten

Ask yourself why you are here, Master Lau had said. The question kept running through Cassidy's head two days later as she sat on the school bleachers in the middle of a Cleary pep rally. Everyone around her was decked out in orange and blue, and they were all clapping and stamping along with the cheers. The entire gym was throbbing with a teeth-rattling beat.

You're here for Eliza, Cassidy reminded herself. Eliza looked great. She was almost beaming with energy and sheer happiness. It was clear that Eliza had every routine down. Even if the decibel level was hurting her head, Cassidy was glad she'd come; she was genuinely happy for her friend.

A huge roar went up after the big finish, a basket toss in which Tamika Foley, the captain of the cheerleaders, landed right on time in perfect formation. Everybody in the gym stood up and cheered as the drummer for the pep band pounded out a quick series of pulsing, rhythmic beats in time to the cheers from the fans: *Go-o-o-o, Warriors!*

As Cassidy got to her feet, she realized that she suddenly felt very tired. She clapped hard, bringing her hands together in time to the beat, and the fatigue grew more intense. She stopped clapping and curled her fingers into a fist. It felt as if the blood had drained from her hands. A weakness began to spread through her arms, shoulders, and then down into her lower body. Her legs trembled slightly, and she hoped she wouldn't fall before getting out of the gym and to the dressing room, where she was supposed to wait for Eliza after the pep rally.

○○○○○

"Are you sure you don't want to come with us, Cassidy?" her mother asked later that evening. "Maybe we shouldn't even go. I don't like the way you look. You're pale."

"She's fine, Wendy," Cassidy's father said.

"Right? You are fine, aren't you? Probably just growing pains."

"Oh, please, Dad. Growing pains?" Cassidy said. "And yes, I'm fine. I'm just kind of tired, that's all. You two go on to Swingside and have a great time."

"We don't really have to," Cassidy's mom said. "It's just that your dad's friend Theo is playing jazz tonight, and we promised we'd be there to sort of bump up the audience for him."

"I'm totally fine with it, Mom, really. Just go already," Cassidy said.

"Maybe I should stay here with Cassidy," Wendy said to Simon.

"Oh, you're not getting off that easy," he said. "I told Theo we'd both be there. Cassidy, I'll have my cell phone on vibrate if you need anything."

"Remember, there's turkey in the fridge for dinner, so make a sandwich, eat something," her mother said as Simon guided her to the door.

Cassidy listened to the sound of the car pulling out of the drive, then turned to her cat. "Well, Monty, it's just you and me tonight," she said. Monty looked up at her and rubbed his furry yellow face against her ankle.

The dark afternoon gloom had developed into an even darker Seattle drizzle, accompanied by an icy wind that seemed to howl around every corner of the Chens' house. Cassidy thought about calling

Eliza but then remembered that she and her mother had gone out of town for the weekend to visit Eliza's grandmother. The evening seemed to press closer, and Cassidy almost wished she had asked her mother to stay home with her. *That's silly,* she told herself. *Stop being such a baby.*

❧❧❧❧❧

Cassidy spent most of the weekend indoors. Her limbs felt heavy, wooden. A couple of times she thought about going outside for a walk—a run was definitely out—but instead she found herself sinking into the sofa to take a nap. Monty stayed close to her, pawing at Cassidy's socks and falling asleep across her feet.

"If you want to stay home today, I'll call school," her mother said on Monday morning.

"No, really, Mom," Cassidy said. "I'll be okay. Besides, I've got a math test tomorrow. I need to get the notes."

❧❧❧❧❧

After what seemed like an endless day of classes, Eliza caught up with Cassidy switching out her books at her locker. "Great, you're still here. I need to stop by Coach Rogers's office and pick up a packet of forms.

Permission slips for the away games, I think. Want to come with?"

Cassidy had been thinking about going home and taking a nap before starting her homework. The day had exhausted her. *This is ridiculous,* she thought. *I'm fourteen—I should have plenty of energy instead of dragging around like I'm half dead.*

"Sure, let's go," Cassidy said with more enthusiasm than she felt. "Let's cut through the auditorium. It's shorter."

The newly renovated Cleary Street Middle School included a state-of-the-art gymnasium that was directly across the courtyard from the older auditorium. The musty smell of the old cloth-covered seats and heavy dark blue stage curtains hit the girls as they took the shortcut through the theater.

Cassidy had a fondness for the old theater space, with its creaky stage and dimly lit corners. A narrow, wooden staircase behind the stage led to an outer door that opened onto the courtyard.

"Creepy," Eliza said as she followed Cassidy down the steep, rickety stairway. "This is like something out of a horror movie. I wouldn't be surprised to find a masked guy with a chain saw waiting for us at the bottom."

"You are such a total drama queen!" Cassidy laughed. "There's nothing scary about these stairs—as long as you don't fall."

Cassidy held on to the smoothly polished wooden banister and then suddenly stopped halfway to the bottom as she felt the oddest sensation. *It couldn't be*—she screamed as she felt the banister move beneath her hand. *It feels—alive!*

She looked down to find her left hand wrapped around the thick body of a gray snake. The serpent writhed in her hand, its muscles shifting beneath its cold scales. Cassidy tried to let go of the snake, but she couldn't loosen her grip.

The head of the snake curled back toward Cassidy's wrist and flicked her lightly with its tongue as if it might be tasting her. And then it bore down on the tender flesh inside her arm. The bite felt as if someone had violently plunged a hypodermic needle into her. The point where the bite entered burned her skin. Cassidy screamed again and looked away but instantly felt her blood grow hot—it felt as if it might be boiling within her veins. She squeezed the snake with all her might, hoping it would crawl through her curled fingers.

"What's wrong?" Eliza cried. "What are you doing?"

SNAP!

The wooden banister broke. The wood clattered to the floor below and echoed in the empty darkness.

Temporarily thrown off balance, Cassidy caught herself just in time. Along with the banister, several support rails had also fallen and lay in a broken heap below. Other rails had been loosened and stood at odd angles, suddenly free of the banister that had held them in place. *It was a snake! I saw it—the banister became a snake—I felt it! It was real! And it bit me!*

As the echo of falling wood faded into the murky shadows, Eliza put her hand on Cassidy's shoulder, steering her away from the exposed edge of the stairs.

"Cassidy, what were you doing?" Eliza asked. "You almost fell! I mean, I saw you . . . like, sort of squeeze and press down on the rail. You squeezed it hard and then it broke!"

"I need to sit down," Cassidy said at last. Her legs felt like putty; she was sure they wouldn't support her much longer.

"Let's get out of here first," Eliza said. She took Cassidy by the arm and helped her to the bottom of the staircase and then outside to the courtyard.

A cold rain was slicing down, and Cassidy didn't protest when Eliza hurried her across the courtyard and back inside the gym. They walked over to a bench near the main door. The boys' basketball team was practicing, their shoes squeaking on the polished floor and the echoes of their calls bouncing like visible energy from the concrete walls.

"Here, let's just sit until you're feeling better," Eliza said, taking charge. "You want some water?"

Cassidy shook her head. "No, I'm okay. I just need to sit a minute." She looked at the inside of her arm. Two small dots of blood had bubbled up to the surface.

"It bit me," she said, her voice quiet. "Eliza, look."

She held out her arm and showed Eliza the two thin lines of blood that had begun to run down the inside of her wrist.

"Bit you?" Eliza asked, and reached into her bag for a tissue. "It splintered—the wood splintered, and then the banister fell. What are you talking about, *it bit you*?"

Eliza must not have seen the snake. She was right there, but she didn't see it. What's wrong with me? Not only did I see the snake, but it really did bite me!

"You want to go see if the school nurse is still here?" Eliza asked.

Cassidy wiped away the blood and saw only two small puncture wounds. She held the tissue tightly against her wrist to stop the bleeding.

"I'm okay, Eliza," Cassidy said after a few minutes of deep breathing. "Let's go pick up your forms or whatever, and then I want to go home."

Eliza didn't move. "What's going on?" she asked. "So much strange stuff has been happening to you lately. It's starting to freak me out."

"This was just an accident," Cassidy said. *How*

can I tell her what I really saw? It doesn't make any sense.

"It didn't exactly look like an accident," Eliza told her. "It looked like you were trying to break the banister."

"I wasn't trying," Cassidy protested, searching for a logical reason for what happened. "I guess when I was holding it, it must have loosened or something — I mean, I felt it sort of move. I guess it was just loose, that's all."

"Come on, Cass, you've got to admit, this is starting to get pretty strange."

Eliza paused, and Cassidy sensed what was coming next. "It's the coins," Eliza said slowly. "That guy at the antiques shop told you they were bad. At first I thought he was crazy, but now I'm starting to believe him."

"No, the coins had nothing to do with this," Cassidy said, refusing to give in to something that sounded so ridiculous. She wasn't even sure who she was trying to convince — Eliza or herself? "It was just an old building trying to kill me."

"I think it's more like the *coins* are trying to kill you," Eliza said.

࿐ ࿐ ࿐ ࿐ ࿐

"I'm calling the principal tomorrow," Simon Chen said that evening at dinner. He was responding to Cassidy's story about the broken banister.

"Mr. Edwards knows, Dad," Cassidy said. "Eliza and I stopped by the office on the way out to get a Band-Aid from the nurse."

"So what did he say?" her mother asked.

"Basically he said that we shouldn't have been taking the shortcut through the theater. He said the auditorium door's supposed to be locked after school. But it's never locked. I've cut through there lots of times, and so do other kids."

"Well, no more shortcuts," Wendy Chen said. "Now eat—you haven't touched a thing on your plate."

"I'm not really hungry," Cassidy said. "Would you mind if I just went up and started my homework?"

"Cassidy, something's wrong," her mother said. "This has gone on too long. You don't have an appetite, you're tired all the time—"

"Maybe you're trying to do too much," her father suggested. "You think you need to cut back on some of your activities?"

"I'm not any busier than usual," Cassidy said. "Maybe it's just a bug or something."

"I think you should stay home tomorrow," her mother said. "I'm going to make an appointment with Dr. Bryant."

"I've got a math test tomorrow!" Cassidy said.

"I hate doing makeups! I've got to be there!"

"You don't have to be there, not until we see what's going on."

"Mom!" Cassidy pleaded.

"Simon, don't you agree that she needs to see the doctor?" asked her mother.

Cassidy looked to her dad, hoping to sway him to her side on this. "I think your mother's right," he said. "It's probably nothing, but it's a good idea to get checked out. You may need to up your vitamins or something simple like that."

"Oh, by the way, Luis called," Wendy said. "He'd like you to call him back right after dinner."

ⓐⓐⓐⓐⓐ

"Hey, Luis," Cassidy said. "Mom said you called."

"Yo, Cass," he said. "Are you coming to Wall Splash tomorrow night? They're having that kung fu festival—and it's one night only."

"I don't know, Luis—I mean, I'd like to go, but I think I'm coming down with something. Mom's making me see the doctor tomorrow."

"Too bad," Luis told her. "Just about everybody from Wing Chun's going—it won't be the same without you there."

Just about everybody? Cassidy thought. *Will James*

be there?

"Who's going?" Cassidy asked, trying to sound casual.

"Well, Brooke said she'd be there—so, score! And Majesta, James, Eric—actually everybody except Shawna and Rico. It's just one night, so nobody wants to miss it."

James was going? That changed everything. "I'll see if I can talk Mom into letting me go," Cassidy said in as casual a tone as she could muster.

She's GOT to let me go! Cassidy thought. *The cutest guy in the world is going to be there!*

෧෧෧෧෧

"I don't know," Cassidy's mom said. "You're going to see the doctor tomorrow, remember?"

"But Mom," Cassidy said. "I'm okay, really. I don't need to see the doctor. There's nothing wrong with me." *Except that I seem to be tired all the time, I'm getting hurt a lot, and I've been having an unusual number of headaches. Oh yeah, and then there's the hallucinations.*

"I don't think so, Cassidy," Wendy said. "But let's see what Dr. Bryant says."

෧෧෧෧෧

Dr. Bryant had been Cassidy's doctor since

she was a baby. Wendy Chen had referred so many Happy Bunny parents to him over the years that he always made time to see Cassidy whenever Wendy called. The waiting room was full of sniffling toddlers and fussy babies. One little girl sat in the chair next to Cassidy and picked at a blue bandage dotted with yellow ducks.

After the checkup Cassidy waited impatiently in Dr. Bryant's office to hear what he had to say. She was barely able to restrain herself from blurting, "So can I go to Wall Splash?"

"Sorry to keep you waiting," the doctor said, "but I'm dealing with a mini–flu epidemic with my little folks. The waiting room's been full for three days now."

He held the folder open in front of him on the desk. "But as for you, Cassidy, everything looks fine. I thought maybe you'd caught the flu bug, too, but now I don't think so. I'm guessing this is a normal back-to-school malady. I see it all the time."

Whew! Cassidy thought, picturing herself sitting close to James at the movie.

"Do you think she should slow down, Dr. Bryant?" Mrs. Chen asked, visibly relieved to hear that there was nothing serious going on. "She's really busy with school this year—lots of homework, plus kung fu."

"What do you think?" he asked, turning to

Cassidy.

She frowned, rubbed her forehead, and slumped forward slightly in her chair. "Yes, Dr. Bryant, I really don't think I should help out at the Happy Bunny anymore. Those little kids exhaust me. I just can't take it anymore."

Wendy rolled her eyes and laughed. "If you feel well enough to make jokes, Cass, you're probably well enough to go back to school. Am I right, Doctor?"

"I'd say so," said Dr. Bryant. "But try to take it easy this week and see how you feel. You can go to school tomorrow, but come right home afterward and get some rest," he said with a smile.

Cassidy groaned. So much for Wall Splash. James would be sitting with Majesta tonight instead.

"If you're still feeling low, come by and we'll see about prescribing an iron supplement or a higher dose of vitamins," he added.

"Just like Dad said," Cassidy told her mother, trying to hide her disappointment.

"Yeah, well, don't tell him or we'll never hear the end of it. Thanks, Dr. Bryant."

ᔕᔕᔕᔕᔕ

On Wednesday morning Cassidy felt no better but was careful not to let her mother know. If she didn't go to school, her mother would never let her go to Wing Chun class. And Cassidy had been thinking of almost nothing except going to Wing Chun class and seeing James again.

Would he say anything about how she was nearly wiped out by the monstrous stretch limo the week before? Did he sit with Majesta at Wall Splash? She had wanted to ask Luis afterward—but couldn't do it. *Why is this happening to me? I should have been there at Wall Splash with my friends—with James!*

The night before, as she'd fallen asleep, she realized that feeling so lousy all the time had left her with a strange, constant sense of dread. It was always there, lying in wait for her just beneath the surface of her thoughts. But seeing James—hoping he'd talk to her, flash that smile at her—was the one thing she looked forward to, the one thing that could make the dread go away.

ⓐ ⓐ ⓐ ⓐ ⓐ

That evening in Wing Chun, almost every one of Cassidy's moves was off. She was paired with Majesta for sticking hands practice and couldn't keep up. Her legs felt heavy, and each movement seemed to take an effort greater than she had to give. Even Master Lau had seemed to notice.

"Aren't you feeling well?" he asked her quietly during one of the drills.

"I'm okay," she said. Showing any kind of weakness seemed out of the question in Master Lau's class. She hoped James didn't notice her pathetic-looking forms.

She left class quickly and waited at the bus stop with Luis. She tried not to notice James standing at the other corner, talking with Majesta, who had been flirting with him every chance she got. This only added to the already-sick feeling that now rested deep in Cassidy's stomach. It was the dread, getting worse by the minute. *It's like something really bad is about to happen and I can't stop it.*

"You're awfully quiet," Luis said as they got on the bus and found seats near the back. "Are you still feeling sick? You got some kind of bug or something?"

"I'm okay," she said. "Just tired, that's all."

"Hey, I heard you're the reason they've started locking the shortcut in the auditorium. Is that right?"

"Yeah, I guess so," she said. "The banister broke the other day."

"That was, like, the quickest way to get to the gym," Luis said.

"Well, too bad, Luis," she said, and it came out sharper than she had intended. "The banister broke and I almost fell. It should be locked."

"Easy, there, klutz-o-matic," Luis told her. "That banister's been there for a long time with no problem, and don't forget that I saw you run into traffic without looking. Is it even safe for me to be sitting with you?"

"Luis, I really don't feel like—" but Cassidy couldn't finish the sentence. The bus was lurching to yet another stop. The fumes seemed to be piped straight into the back window where she sat. "I really don't feel so hot. I just want to get home," she said.

"Sure, we're almost there," Luis said. "Sorry, Cass, I didn't know it was that bad. You want me to walk you up to your door?"

Cassidy looked up to see that the bus had finally reached her stop. "No, I'll be okay. Thanks anyway, Luis, and sorry I kind of yelled at you."

"No prob. Feel better, okay?"

Easier said than done, Cassidy thought as she walked toward the front of the bus, feeling that each step took more energy than she had left.

🌸 *Chapter Eleven*

Cassidy missed school on Thursday. She spent the entire day in bed, sleeping, dreaming weird dreams about the two women again. This time the women stood at the foot of her bed and said, *Don't give in. Remember that you are a warrior. The demon is present. You must be strong.*

Her mother brought a bowl of chicken soup to her for lunch. "Your dad's picking up some kind of industrial-strength vitamins for you."

"That's great, Mom," Cassidy said. "Thanks for staying home with me today."

Her mother pushed Cassidy's hair out of her face and smiled. "Are you kidding? I needed a break, too. We should do this more often. Well, not get sick, of course, but maybe take more time for ourselves."

"Definitely," Cassidy agreed. "Have you seen Monty?"

Monty had been curled next to Cassidy most of the morning while she slept. "Downstairs, I guess," her mom replied. "I was heating the soup and he came tearing around the corner like something was after him. Last time I saw him, he was in the laundry basket."

ᘒᘒᘒᘒᘒ

On Friday Cassidy went back to school. The fluorescent light tubes down the hallways and in the classrooms burned her eyes. The sounds of bells and loudspeaker announcements were shrill and sent waves of nausea through her. By lunchtime she felt completely wiped out.

"Would you look at this vitamin?" Cassidy said. She held open her hand and showed Eliza the dark green and brown speckled capsule.

"Want me to wrap it up in a piece of bread and feed it to you?" Eliza asked her. "That's how we used to give our dog his vitamins."

"Gee, thanks for the offer," Cassidy said. "What a great friend . . . but no." Cassidy put the huge, nasty-smelling vitamin in her mouth and then swallowed almost an entire carton of milk. "That's awful!" she sputtered. "This stuff better help."

"You know what they say," Eliza said, biting into a chicken wrap, "what doesn't kill you makes you stronger!"

❧❧❧❧❧

"I made an appointment for you to see Patrick Healy today," Wendy said during breakfast the next morning. "He's the healer Sarah Clifford's been seeing."

"She has a healer named Patrick *Healy*?" Simon asked, looking at Cassidy with a huge grin on his face and raised eyebrows. "Can anybody spell *quack*?"

"He's not a quack, Simon," Cassidy's mother said. "It's impossible to get an appointment with this guy, and Sarah's giving up her time slot so that Cassidy can get in."

"Mom," Cassidy said warily, "is this some kind of New Agey thing? I mean, Mrs. Clifford's been doing all kinds of meditation poses and chugging herbal drinks."

Then, without missing a beat, Simon looked at Cassidy and quacked like a duck.

❧❧❧❧❧

Patrick Healy opened the door and peered out at the crowd of people in his tiny waiting room. He had a large, reddish face with red hair pulled back into a thick ponytail that hung long to his waist. "Cassidy Chen?" he asked.

Cassidy and her mother followed Patrick Healy into a small, square room with a white-draped table in the middle and several plastic chairs along the edges of the walls.

"Thanks so much for seeing us today, Dr. Healy," Mrs. Chen began.

"Not a doctor," he interrupted. "Call me Patrick."

In the next few minutes Patrick Healy looked at the inside of Cassidy's nose and mouth and then tapped several times on her knees and the bottoms of her feet with a small rubber hammer. He put a big red hand on the top of her head as if he might be palming a basketball and closed his eyes for a full minute.

"You taking vitamins?" he asked.

"Yes," Cassidy answered.

"Thought so," he said, smiling as if he was proud of himself. "Everything's kind of cranked up in there. Vitamins make you just hum, man. It's wild."

"Uh, okay," Cassidy said, wondering if that was supposed to be good or bad.

"Anyway, here's the deal. Your whole balance thing, your yin and yang, is way off. Yin is dark and yang is light, right? Well, yours is like . . ." He seemed to be searching for the right words. "Yours is whacked out of balance—way whacked out."

"I'm not sure I understand," Cassidy's mom said. "I mean, what's causing the . . . the, ah, yin and yang to—"

Patrick Healy ignored her, his attention focused on Cassidy. "Don't take this personally," he said, "but I have to ask. Have you had any problems with the spirit world lately? Have you been cursed or something?"

"Cursed?" Wendy practically shouted. "What are you talking about? We came here because she gets really tired. We thought maybe there would be some herbal remedy to boost her energy level. And now you're asking if she's been cursed?"

Patrick Healy held up his hands defensively. "Ease up, ma'am. I just call it like I see it." He turned back to Cassidy. "Bet you've had a bunch of accidents lately, too, am I right?"

Too stunned to speak, Cassidy just nodded.

"Your yin-yang gets out of whack that bad, look out."

"Cassidy, put on your shoes—we're leaving," Mrs. Chen said curtly.

"Meditate," Patrick advised as Cassidy left the office—practically shoved out by her mother. "Surround yourself with light."

"Can you believe that?" Wendy said as they

stepped out of Healy's office and into the busy downtown hustle of a Seattle Saturday. "A curse?"

"Definitely weird," Cassidy said. *But is it all that weird?* she wondered. *A lot of what Healy the Healer just said about the accidents and balance sort of made sense.*

Which led to a scary question: Had she been cursed?

❧ Chapter Twelve

Master Lau's studio was often drafty and chilly, but the weather had changed, and now it was positively cold. So no one thought anything of it when Cassidy wore her long-sleeved tee and long sweats to hide the bruises that blossomed on her skin at even the slightest pressure.

There were four angry-looking marks the size of fingertips on her left forearm where Luis had grabbed her during a Wing Chun drill the previous week. Even Monty, jumping into her lap one night, had left purplish bruises the size of cat's paws on her upper legs. But the bruises, Cassidy realized, were just the visible signs that something else was going on.

She tried to control the weakness she felt with breathing exercises she'd learned in Wing Chun. And when the pain behind her eyes became too intense, she tried to meditate, as Patrick Healy had suggested, until the pain gradually dissolved. But it was always there—like a poison slowly coursing through her body.

After warm-ups that seemed to go on forever, Master Lau paired the students for sticking hands. "You, Mr. Tang," Master Lau said to James, who stood with his arms crossed, "you practice *chi sau* today with Ms. Chen." As Master Lau continued around the circle, pairing the students, James ambled over to Cassidy's side.

Cassidy couldn't believe her luck. She was finally getting to practice with James.

"Remember to pay attention to the elbow and the wrist," Master Lau said. "You will feel energy, or what we call commitment to fight, at these points."

Cassidy faced James and took in a deep breath. Suddenly her nerves set in. He was so good-looking, it was distracting. And if she wanted to impress him with her prowess, she'd need all the concentration she could muster.

As she took a moment to prepare, Cassidy commanded herself to focus. She moved in a slow circle to the right, careful to keep both arms in near proximity to James's arms without actually touching. She watched his eyes, looking for even the slightest change, for anything that might warn her of his next move. James, though, was impossible to read. He moved with her, step for step, a half-amused, half-bored look on his face, which she found totally disconcerting. When he grabbed her wrist, she was supposed to be ready for it, to anticipate it. But she wasn't—probably because of his incredible brown eyes that followed her every move. She failed to execute the *bong sau* move in which she was supposed to bring up her elbow to block his hand.

They resumed their slow circling, Cassidy now fiercely determined to keep up, to show him that she was good at this, too. She leaned in close with her elbow, and he responded immediately by dropping his arm slightly into a *tan sao*, or upper side block, then deflecting her arm, which sent a spasm of pain up to her shoulder. *He is scary good*, she thought. *I am so out of my league with this guy—how does he make it look so easy?*

Frustrated by his lightning-fast reflexes and the impossible way he seemed to anticipate her every move, she finally asked, "Am I boring you?"

He cracked a smile but kept moving. "Nah," he said, "Just like keeping you on your toes."

Is he flirting with me? Cassidy wondered. She kind of thought he was but quickly corrected herself.

That would be too good to be true.

James continued moving effortlessly, soundlessly, and Cassidy did her best to keep up. *It's like a dance*, she thought. *First you lead, then I do. Our feet never stepping too close or too far apart. Our arms only a breath's distance from each other, waiting for the next move.*

Cassidy stepped to the left and then right, and as James followed, she made contact with his wrist. He made the proper move to block but was a fraction of a second too slow, allowing her to move in for the grab.

"Nice work, Cassidy," Master Lau said. Surprised, Cassidy nodded her thanks. She'd had no idea that Master Lau was watching.

As Master Lau walked back to the front of the class to dismiss them for the evening, Cassidy stole a glance at James, almost involuntarily. He smiled at her and mouthed the words, "Nice job, Crane Girl." *Is he teasing me? No, he's flirting with me—I'm sure of it.*

⌁⌁⌁⌁⌁

By the end of class, Cassidy was thoroughly exhausted. Even putting on her jacket and gloves seemed to require superhuman effort, and she was the last one out of the studio.

Hoping she wouldn't have to wait too long for a bus, she stepped out onto the street. James was waiting a few doors down in front of the newsstand. Cassidy's breath caught. This was her chance. They'd just done sticking hands together; she had an excuse to talk to him. But what should she say? During *chi sau*, it had almost seemed as if James could read her mind. *Does that mean he can tell that I like him? Should I wait for some kind of signal?*

"There you are," she heard him say. But James wasn't looking in Cassidy's direction. She followed his eyes toward the newsstand. Majesta was walking out of the store with a bottle of orange juice in her hand. Majesta, supermodel gorgeous, walked toward James with a confidence that Cassidy could never imagine feeling.

"Ready to ride?" he asked.

"I'm always ready," Majesta answered.

James reached into his jacket pocket and pulled out a set of keys, holding them up in front of Majesta.

Cassidy had stopped, frozen in place. Almost as if he sensed her, James turned in her direction. "Hey, Cass," he said easily. "Need a ride? I've got my dad's car tonight."

Cassidy saw the quickest flicker of a look on Majesta's face. A look that absolutely screamed, *No, Cassidy Chen, you do NOT want a ride with James Tang.*

But before she could answer, Luis waved from the opposite corner. "Cassidy, move it already!" he shouted. "The bus just turned the corner. Are you coming or not?"

"I'm coming, Luis," she called.

Feeling a sickness in the pit of her stomach that increased with each step, Cassidy walked up to James. "Thanks, but I'm taking the bus tonight," she explained.

"Sure, later," he said.

"See you next week, Cass," Majesta called out as Cassidy crossed the street to join Luis at the bus stop.

See you next week, Cass. Cassidy hated the superior tone Majesta had used. She said the words exactly the way, Cassidy imagined, an older sister might speak to her much-younger sister.

ᗧᗧᗧᗧᗧ

Will this bus ride never end? Cassidy wondered. The bus crawled through snarled traffic, and Luis babbled on and on about Brooke. "You know, she's pretty good at Wing Chun, have you noticed?"

Cassidy had been looking out the bus window and saw that a steady rain had started falling. Her shoulder ached from the sticking hands drill with James.

"Hey," Luis said, bumping against her, "are you even listening to me?" The slight jolt was enough to send a tremor of razor-sharp barbs through Cassidy's right arm.

"Stop it, Luis!" she snapped, rubbing her arm. "That hurt!"

"Sorry," he said. "But Cassidy, haven't you noticed—you hardly listen to anything I say anymore. Is it because of James? Do you *like* him or something?"

"You're crazy," Cassidy said, and looked toward the front of the bus, wishing the traffic would move.

"I don't think so, Cass," Luis continued. "You act . . . different around him."

Cassidy's face burned. *Is it that obvious? Is it obvious to James?*

"And you don't think you act different around Brooke?" she shot back without thinking. "You've been rattling on and on about Brooke, but she has absolutely zero interest in you, okay?"

As soon as the words were out, Cassidy was sorry, but it was too late. Several people turned around to see who was raising her voice at the back of the bus. Luis looked at Cassidy with dark eyes that couldn't hide how deeply her words had cut him. He didn't say anything but picked up his messenger bag and walked toward the front. She saw him say something to the driver, who then pulled over to the curb and let him off even though it wasn't one of the scheduled stops.

Cassidy watched him from her window. Luis slung the strap of his bag over his shoulder and began a slow walk toward Fremont with his head down. The bus pulled away from the curb, and Cassidy saw the glittering lights of the city turn to water as she peered out through the October drizzle that covered Seattle like a curse.

✿ Chapter Thirteen

The red latex faces of at least a dozen sneering demons swung from hooks just inches above Cassidy's head. Pop's Clowns & More, a cavernous warehouse famous for stocking every kind of horror imaginable, was filled with shoppers searching for the perfect Halloween costume.

"It's gotta be something unique," Eliza was saying, fingering the gossamer white fabric of a princess costume. "Tamika didn't have to invite us to this party, you know. It's really her brother Ned's Halloween party. Mostly Wilder High students."

Eliza was on overdrive, and Cassidy didn't want to tell her how totally uninterested she was in the party, finding the perfect costume, or getting to know any high school friends of Ned Foley. She was more interested in making up with her own friend, Luis. But so far he still wasn't speaking to her at school and hadn't answered any of her e-mails or phone calls.

"I wish we'd had a little more notice," Cassidy said. For Eliza's sake, she was trying to muster some enthusiasm for the task of choosing the right costumes for Tamika and Ned's party, which was less than a week away.

"What about this?" Cassidy asked. She held up a devil's costume for Eliza to inspect. The costume's skirt was made up of several thin layers of orange, red, and yellow satin so that when it moved, it resembled flames. "Look, it even comes with horns and a pitchfork. We could go as devil twins. What about it?"

Eliza shook her head after no more than a glance. "Too cliché," she said.

"Vampires? Werewolves? Zombies?" Cassidy asked, glancing up at the ceiling, where the empty-eyed faces dripped blood and gore from their realistic-looking wounds.

"'Lions and tigers and bears, oh my!'" Eliza said, laughing. "Let's ask the guy where the Oz stuff is."

"Right," said Cassidy. "'Follow the yellow brick road.'"

"Look—over there," Eliza said. She held a blue-and-white-checked Dorothy dress up to her neck. "What do you think, Cass? Remember that girl on the Oz Tones video? I mean, she had the bared tummy and the tattoos, but it was definitely a Dorothy dress and she looked amazing."

"Love the ruby slippers," Cassidy told her. "And you can braid your own hair—you won't even need the wig. In fact, the wig's kind of ratty-looking, anyway."

"Perfect," said Eliza with a satisfied nod at her reflection in the mirror. "Okay, my costume's all settled. Now, how about you? Wicked witch or good witch?"

There it is again, Cassidy thought. *Yin and yang. Dark and light. Good and evil.*

Cassidy held the wicked witch costume in front of her and looked in the mirror. It even came with a crooked, warty nose and some adhesive to fix it in place. Then she looked at the good witch costume, with its shimmering gown of pale blue and white and the silver magic wand with its chipped paint and cheap-looking plastic streamers.

"I don't think so." Cassidy shook her head. "Unless I'm with you the entire night, who's gonna even know my costume's part of the Oz thing? I'll just look like a witch or else a fairy godmother."

"Yeah, I see what you mean," Eliza said. "Maybe the Tin Man?"

"Forget it—I'm not wearing that thing all night long." Cassidy laughed, thumping the plastic shell of the Tin Man costume. And before Eliza could get the words out of her mouth, Cassidy stopped her. "And you can forget the lion and that dum-dum who needs a brain. You're going to look so hot in your tiny little Dorothy costume. I don't want to wear anything that makes me look stupid—or fat!"

"Then I guess this costume is out, too?" Eliza asked. She held up a huge emerald green velvet frock coat worn by the powerful and almighty Oz.

"Let's keep looking, Dorothy," Cassidy said.

ଛ ଛ ଛ ଛ ଛ

"I guess this must be it," Mrs. Chen said, pulling the car up to the curb. Tamika's family lived in a large gray stone house that rested atop a sprawling patch of green. The neatly trimmed lawn sloped down to the street on the west side, and Cassidy could see beyond the house to the edge of Discovery Park, which bordered the property to the north. Grinning pumpkins lined the slate walk up to the front door, covered in a lacy network of fake spiderwebs.

A guy wearing a plastic Viking hat and a girl in a genie costume, complete with pierced belly button, walked past the Chens' car on their way to the party. "Do you know those two?" Mrs. Chen asked.

"No, Mom, they're probably friends of Tamika's

brother," Cassidy said. "I guess Eliza and I should go in now."

"Remember, I'll be waiting right here at eleven. On the dot, do you hear me? And you have the cell phone with you so if anything gets out of hand or if you need me to come back early, just call."

"Right, Mom," Cassidy said. "And we'll stick together and look out for each other and basically try to have as little fun as possible, okay?"

"Don't worry, Mrs. Chen," Eliza reassured Wendy. "If I have to, I'll just click my heels together three times and say, 'There's no place like home.'"

"Very funny, Dorothy," Mrs. Chen said. "Okay. I guess I'm overreacting. I mean, these high school kids are only a year older than you. . . . All right, you're released," she said rather reluctantly. "Go, have a sensible amount of fun, and I'll see you at eleven."

Eliza and Cassidy stepped out of the car and straightened their costumes before starting up the walk.

"Cassidy, I know I keep gushing, but really, you look amazing," Eliza said. "I am so totally jealous. I feel like an overgrown farm girl in my Dorothy dress and you—you're this mysterious, like, woodsy goth girl or something!"

When Cassidy hadn't been able to find anything she liked at Pop's costume shop, she decided to make her own costume. She remembered a story she'd read to the kids at the Happy Bunny about the wood fairies who lived beneath the forest floor among the gnarled roots of ancient trees and decided a wood fairy was what she wanted to be.

Cassidy had woven a long tangle of brown and green moss into her own hair. Then her mother had used temporary hair dye to paint in streaks of browns, golds, and deep greens that shimmered now under the dim streetlight.

Wendy had also painted Cassidy's face with glittery gold and green fairy streaks and swirls. The bright dust above her eyes and across her cheeks gave Cassidy's face a dark, mysterious glow.

Her dress was a fitted brown top and a long flowing skirt made from diaphanous strips of brown and green that swirled around her ankles as she walked. Tendrils of green silk ivy that had been woven in her hair curled around her neck and then looped over her right shoulder and down her arm, ending at her fingertips, where even her fingernails were painted brown and green.

"Par-ty," Eliza said as she and Cassidy walked up the cement path that led to Tamika's front door. But before Eliza could knock at the spiderwebbed door, it swung open, letting the thrumming strains of a serious guitar solo pour out, covering Dorothy and the wood fairy in its soulful, walloping beat.

"Aaaar! Mateys!" bellowed an extremely cute pirate wearing dreadlocks and an eye patch. Tamika, a bouncy, 1950s teenybopper in a poodle skirt and ponytail, rescued Cassidy and Eliza at the door, introducing them first to her brother Ned, the pirate.

Most of the party was taking place in the kitchen, which opened into a large room at the back of the house with a wall of windows and French doors that looked out over a spacious lawn. Outside, several people stood around in small clusters, drinking from plastic cups and eating slivers of pizza under twinkling orange pumpkin lights that hung from the low branches of trees.

"Great party, Tamika," Eliza said.

"Thanks. Food's in the kitchen—help yourself. And FYI, you may see the folks lurking around tonight," Tamika said with a wave. Once she was gone, it became painfully clear to Cassidy that other than Eliza, the party was void of any familiar faces.

"Oz Tone fan?" a voice said. Cassidy and Eliza turned to see a tall scarecrow with real straw sticking out of the collar and cuffs of his checked shirt. Cassidy had no idea who it was.

"Ben?" Eliza asked. "From Hip Hop?"

Ooh, that Ben.

"Yeah," he said. "You remembered. And you're, what, a dance class drop-out or something? You came to, like, two classes and that was it?"

Eliza shrugged. "I got too busy with cheerleading."

"So are you an Oz Tone fan? Because if

you're supposed to be Dorothy, you're missing some tattoos."

"Yeah, well, I like the music video anyway," Eliza said.

Cassidy decided to leave Eliza and Ben to their bubble of bliss and went in search of something cool to drink. The room was full of people, and the pulsing music seemed to generate even more heat.

In the kitchen about a dozen people stood around a table littered with open pizza boxes and plastic cups. She didn't see anyone she recognized and really didn't feel like starting a conversation with a total stranger. Maybe she would just grab something to drink and then see if she could find Eliza.

Cassidy poured a cup of soda from a two-liter bottle on the table. When she looked up, she saw Majesta sweep through the door dressed like a Greek goddess in a silky white dress and gold sash. *Great, the only person I know here is the very person I'd prefer least to know.*

Majesta had brought a date, some guy dressed as Zorro in a black cape, a black hat pulled low over his face, and a mask over his eyes.

"Guys, my friend James," Majesta said. "James, meet the dregs of society from Wilder High, brought together tonight by that swashbuckling pirate over there, Ned."

James nodded and lifted the mask up over his

eyes.

Cassidy couldn't believe what she saw. *James? James Tang is here as Majesta's date?* She began to back up, hoping to melt unseen into the kitchen wall. Cassidy had loved her wood fairy costume but now felt like a dumpy character from a production of children's theater next to movie star–like Majesta in her clingy white and gold dress.

A breath of fresh air and a moment to talk herself down was what Cassidy needed. So she quietly inched her way toward the door and snuck out. But just as she stepped outside, she felt a tap on her shoulder. "I thought that was you," James said. "Great costume, Cassidy. Guess you're going to frolic in the forest now?"

"Not exactly," Cassidy said. "I just needed some fresh air."

"Same here," James said. "This Zorro thing is, like, unbelievably hot."

"Tell me about it. No one warned me that dressing like a wood fairy involved sweat—"

"James!" Majesta called from the door, cutting short Cassidy's alone time with James. The silvery moon bathed the lawn in soft light and illuminated the whiteness of Majesta's dress as she glided over to where James and Cassidy stood. "There you are. Oh, hi, Cass. Cute costume, and you are a . . . no, don't tell me, I love guessing. A shrub?"

"She's a wood fairy," James said. "From an Irish folktale, right, Cass?"

"Right," Cassidy said, impressed that he knew the story.

"Let's go in, James, I want to introduce you to one of my best friends from Wilder," Majesta said, taking his arm.

"You coming in, Cass?" James asked her.

"In a minute," she answered. "It feels pretty good out here."

Cassidy waited until James and Majesta were back inside, and then she went over to the windows and looked into the large room. She saw Eliza standing in a corner, still talking to the scarecrow. Cassidy waved her hands until Eliza looked up, and then she motioned for Eliza to meet her at the door.

"Party's great, huh, Cass? Erin and Chrissy just got here. They're devil twins. Come on inside," Eliza said, looking out over the shadowy lawn. "What are you doing out here, anyway, hiding in the trees or something?"

"I'm not hiding," Cassidy said. "It's just—well, guess who's here with Majesta—as her *date*!"

"James? The guy from your Wing Chun class?"

"Yeah, they're in the kitchen."

"I want to see him. What does he look like?"

"He looks like Zorro right now," Cassidy said.

"And Majesta looks gorgeous, as usual. She's dressed like a goddess." Cassidy couldn't stop thinking about Majesta asking her whether she was a shrub.

"Don't let them ruin the party for you, Cass," Eliza said. "Let's try to have a good time. Ben's really funny, and there are some other people here from Cleary Street that you know."

Someone turned up the music, and Eliza was practically shouting to be heard. *I can't go in there. I can't run into James and Majesta again,* Cassidy thought.

"I'll be in soon, Eliza," she said. "I'm just going to cool off, and then I'll catch up with you."

As Cassidy walked over to a low bench near a cluster of evergreens, she noticed her eyes burning. *Probably from the glitter makeup,* she thought.

When she sat down, she felt a scratchy burning at the back of her throat that extended deep into her lungs. Aching with a tiredness that was beyond anything she'd experienced before, she felt as heavy and lifeless as the stone beneath her.

The image of James and Majesta together played itself again and again in her head. *His smile. The way she took his arm.*

A slight shift in darkness caused her to look up to see the moon slide behind a thin veil of dark clouds. *Great, now it's going to rain. Perfect. Could my life get any worse?*

Cassidy was tired of pretending that everything

was okay when clearly it wasn't.

She looked toward the house, which glowed with light and life. The bright colors of the costumes ran together and merged in a dancing rainbow. The music and the voices spilled out of the house, and though Cassidy wanted to be drawn into it, to become a part of it—she couldn't. *I'm . . . not like them.* Why did she feel so different? What was happening to her? *I've got to get out of here. I've got to leave.*

And as soon as she thought it, she knew that was what she had to do. She couldn't stand to stay one more minute in the shadows of a party where everybody was laughing and having fun. And there was absolutely no way she could go inside and pretend that she was having a great time—she just didn't have the energy to pretend. She had to leave.

Twinkling lights bordered a small path through the garden to a heavy iron gate set in the middle of the stone wall. Beyond the wall was a heavily wooded area of Discovery Park. *A quiet forest with no people, no Majesta and James, no pretending.* Cassidy followed the lights down the path to the gate, feeling around for a handle, hoping it wouldn't be locked. She found a rusty latch, and it creaked eerily as she lifted it and then swung open the gate.

❧ Chapter Fourteen

Stepping into the dense forest was like entering another world. The muted sounds of the music from the party were gone. In fact, Cassidy noticed, there was very little sound at all except for the noise her boots made as she walked through the dried leaves. Damp smells of pine and earth rose from the forest floor and hung thick in the air. She soon found herself on a path that curved to the left and then descended in a gradual slope.

As Cassidy continued down the path, she saw something flickering up ahead. *Candles? Flashlights?*

Are those really lights, or am I seeing things? Is someone out there? Her eyes felt blurry again, and her head began to throb.

But the lights still called to her, and Cassidy was curiously aware that she felt almost unable to look the other way. *I should go back to the party,* she told herself. *This is crazy.* But at the same time she kept walking down the sloping, muddy path as the forest gloom closed in around her. *Why can't I turn back?* It felt as if someone, or something, called to her.

Or is it a song? She stopped to listen and heard a beautiful voice that hummed and beckoned her toward the lights. She felt helpless to resist as she continued down the path. Rain had started to fall, tapping out a rush of whispered secrets against the leafy canopy of the trees. The path now was becoming even more muddy and slippery with fallen leaves and pine needles, but it wasn't enough to turn her back. Not with the promise of the song leading her closer to the flickering lights.

Finally she reached a small clearing where dozens of small stone lanterns containing burning candles glittered in the eerie forest gloom. The song grew faint and ended on a long and sorrowful note that faded away in the darkness. *Who's out there?* Cassidy wondered. *Who lit all these candles?*

The rain fell harder, and Cassidy was doubled over with a coughing fit. Putting her hand to her mouth, she realized she was burning up with fever.

It's the fever, she thought. *I'm hallucinating. I'm hearing things.*

Suddenly there was a fluttery sound with a slight metallic ring to it. *Definitely not a bird or bat.* Cassidy stared into the darkness.

I need to get out of here, she thought. She wanted to run, but there was no way she could go quickly through the dense forest in the dark.

She heard the fluttering sound again. It was closer now and seemed to sense her movement toward what she had hoped was the path. Was it possible that whatever was making the sound could see her? Was it tracking her?

She wanted to scream but was afraid that any noise she made might draw whatever was out there straight toward her. *Besides, no one will hear me. I'm too far from the house, and nobody even knows I'm out here.*

Before one can fight, one must learn to stand. Words from Master Lau, but could they help her now? Cassidy took a deep breath and tried to find her balance. Was it possible that she could use her Wing Chun skills in defending herself against whatever seemed to be circling her?

Self-defense is like a mirror, Master Lau had once told his students. *It responds to what is before it.*

The metallic fluttering sounded again, and this time, thanks to the moon's light, Cassidy could actually see what was making the unearthly noise. It was a large white snake, lifted by scaly, paper-thin wings, and it was flying straight toward her.

Chapter Fifteen

The creature's wings beat the air hard, creating a silvery slick sound that sliced through the darkness. *This can't be real! This is not happening!* Whether it was her Wing Chun training or just a simple survival instinct, Cassidy raised her arms to the correct position, ready to deflect the first strike.

The creature hung in the air in front of her face, supported by two razor-sharp wings blurred by their speedy flapping. *It's waiting for me to make a move.* If only she didn't feel so weak. They circled each other in a bizarre version of some Wing Chun drill gone wrong.

I'm getting weaker, Cassidy realized. *And this . . . this . . . grotesque . . . creature . . . or whatever it is knows I'm too weak to fight.* In that instant, as if the winged creature had read her mind, it attacked. Mouth open, fangs bared, it moved in for the kill.

Cassidy blocked the first strike with her forearm, but the snake turned quickly and looped itself around her neck. She grabbed it just behind the head to keep it from sinking its fangs into her — but she felt a tightening at her throat. *This is it,* she realized. *I can't fight. It's strangling me!* She sank to her knees on the muddy ground and closed her eyes, unable to breathe as the snake tightened its grip. *Oh my God, I'm going to die right here in the forest!*

Suddenly there was a release and she could breathe again. As she filled her lungs with sweet, precious air, she saw someone fling the creature to the ground and then pull a sword from a scabbard at his waist.

It was James.

The snake hit the forest floor hard but quickly rebounded. With a powerful flick of its tail, the snake yanked the sword from James's hand. The weapon flew up into the darkness of night, reflecting moonlight before clattering back to earth.

Cassidy ran for the sword, grabbed it with both hands, and raised it high overhead. As the snake flew toward her, she brought the sword down with a strength that surprised her. She felt the smooth, awful sensation of the blade slicing effortlessly through flesh. The snake fell to the ground in a bloody, unmoving coil. The sheer metallic wings curled in and dried into brittle flakes before blowing away like silvery dust in the slight breeze. As Cassidy and James watched in disbelief, the creature shriveled and turned gray until soon it looked like any other dead snake that might be found in the woods.

What just happened? This feels straight out of Final Fantasy! Cassidy took a deep, cleansing breath and for the first time in a long time, she didn't feel a throbbing ache in her bones or a dizzying spell of nausea.

She needed answers. "James, what . . ."

"Not now." He shook his head. "There's no time."

James wiped the blade of the sword with a handful of wet leaves. He replaced the sword in its case and took Cassidy by the hand. "We need to get back. Your friend's looking for you. We'll talk later."

🌸 Chapter Sixteen

The moonlight cast shadows of skeletal trees as Cassidy followed James back down the narrow path. Before stepping out of the woods, he turned to her. He had removed his mask, and Cassidy was astonished at the intensity of his eyes. "Are you okay?"

"Yeah . . . but how did you know I was in the park?" Cassidy asked.

"I heard your friend ask if anybody had seen you. I went outside to cool off and happened to notice the gate was open—not smart, Cassidy, to go off like that by yourself into a city park at night."

Ironic . . . since you're the reason I left the party in the first place, Cassidy mused. *And there's no way to explain that something was . . . was calling me into the forest.*

Muted sounds from the party began to reach them as James pushed open the iron gate. "We went for a walk, okay?" he said to Cassidy. "That's all anybody needs to know right now."

The gate creaked shut behind them, the rusted latch falling into place, as if declaring an end to their conversation.

"Cassidy!" Eliza called from the patio.

"I'm here, Eliza," Cassidy called out. "We're coming."

Eliza looked from Cassidy to James and then back again. "I couldn't find you anywhere," she said. "I was worried."

"Sorry. I . . . well, we decided to go for a walk," Cassidy said, feeling the lie hang in the air, as transparent as the mist that settled over them.

Eliza was silent for a moment, a confused Dorothy waking up at the end of a bad dream. "It's almost eleven. Your mom's parked out front."

"I should go in and thank Tamika," Cassidy said.

"I already thanked her for both of us," Eliza said. "And by the way," she added, turning to James, "Majesta's looking for you."

 @@@@@

On the drive home Eliza managed to keep up the conversation for both of them.

"Nobody really *got* my Oz Tones costume," Eliza said. "Except for Ben. He's really pretty cool — I'm kind of bummed that I ditched the dance classes now."

"Did they have food?" Wendy asked. "Did you get to eat something?"

"Yeah, the usual stuff — pizza that was pretty bad and some soggy sandwiches," Eliza answered. "Oh yeah, some kind of orange punch in this huge plastic skull. Did you have any punch, Cassidy? It was actually pretty good."

"No, I didn't notice the punch," she said. *I was too busy fighting a snake . . . or, more specifically, a winged snake that attacked me in the forest.* When James had thrown it to the ground, the snake had coiled into a tight spring, wings extended, preparing to strike again. As Cassidy continued thinking about the snake incident, something dawned on her. Something so obvious, it was a wonder she hadn't thought about it before. The engraving on the first coin was a snake.

"So, anyway, thanks for the ride home," Eliza said as Mrs. Chen pulled into a parking space in front of her apartment building. "Cass, let's get together tomorrow, okay? Catch up?" Cassidy had no trouble making an instant, silent translation of this: *I want to know why you disappeared from the party for such a long time and then reappeared with James Tang.*

ഗഗഗഗഗ

"I take it you both had a good time?" her mother asked as they continued on home. "You're kind of quiet. Everything okay? You're not feeling sick again, Cassidy?"

"I feel fine, Mom," she said.

"I'm so glad you had a good time," Wendy said, easing the car into the garage. "And I'm glad you're feeling better, too. Maybe your dad was right—you were just experiencing some growing pains."

In the glare of the bright overhead garage light, Cassidy saw a couple of small, iridescent scales caught in the gauzy weave of her wood fairy dress. "Yeah, Mom, growing pains. Dad was probably right."

ഗഗഗഗഗ

Back in her room, Cassidy examined herself in the mirror. Her glittery green and gold face held no clue of the ferocious battle she had been in. Rubbing her forearms, she wondered if there would be a lot of bruises—to join all the other bruises that had been forming at the slightest touch during the past weeks.

The only way to find out would be to shower off the paint and mud. As Cassidy began to peel away the damp layers of her wood fairy costume, Monty came into her room and sniffed at the green and brown fabric.

"What's up with you, Monty?" Cassidy said, reaching down to pick him up in her arms. He rubbed his head against her cheek as if trying to wipe away the green and brown face paint. "It's still me," she said. Monty looked up at her, peering deeply into her eyes, and Cassidy could swear he understood what she had been through.

∾∾∾∾∾

Stepping out of the shower, she looked into the mirror again. In addition to the old purplish bruises that still marked her body, there was a redness, almost like a scuff mark, around her neck where the snake had tried to strangle her. On her forearm a small crescent-shaped cut was marked by a thin line of dried blood. She remembered deflecting the first strike and seeing a razor-sharp wing slash the air before coming in contact with her arm.

What's happening to me? The fall on the steps, the banister, the limo, and then the strange sickness. And now, fighting with some kind of snake creature that can't possibly exist. That looked like the snake picture on one of the gold coins. Isn't it a bit insane to keep ruling out the possibility that all of these events are somehow related to the coins?

Cassidy retrieved the box and shuffled through the coins until she found the one engraved with the winged snake. *It's glowing,* she realized, rubbing the surface. *The coin is actually warm.* She closed her hand around it, squeezing it in her palm and feeling an intense heat as the coin's pale light spilled out between her fingers.

She opened her hand and looked closely at the winged snake. *I've got to find out what's going on before it happens again. Who knows? Maybe I was just lucky this time.* She thought about the jade dog charm her dad had given her for luck. She also thought about the fairy dust her great-grandmother had once used to make good luck charms. *I need all the good luck I can get.*

"You still up, Cassidy?" her mother called from outside the door.

"Uh, yeah, Mom, I showered off the paint and gunk from the costume. I'm going to bed soon," she said, pushing the box of coins underneath her pillow.

"Sleep well," her mother said, leaning into the room.

"Night, Mom, and thanks for taking us to the party."

"No problem. See you in the morning, princess."

Princess? Hearing the word reminded her of the dream from her fourteenth birthday. *The two women who called me Mingmei said that I was a warrior princess.*

That I'm destined to fight five evil spirits in order to fulfill some destiny and that the spirits would try to destroy me, but an ally would find me.

Then she thought of James pulling the snake from her neck. He had shown up just in time — *Was the snake the evil spirit? Is James the ally?*

Cassidy fell asleep under the slanted golden moonlight that slipped through her window and covered her like a pale blanket. As she drifted off, she was faintly aware that Monty was still awake and watching, his whiskers twitching, tasting the air to see what had changed.

∞∞∞∞∞

"Salad?" Cassidy asked Eliza the next day at lunch. "Or we could order a pizza. Mom left some money." Almost as if she had sensed the moment Cassidy's parents had left the house, Eliza had called Cassidy and not-so-subtly invited herself over.

"Definitely salad," Eliza said with a moan. "Did you eat any of that nasty pizza at the party last night? It was like toxic pie or something. Oh, of course you didn't have any pizza because you weren't really *at* the party, were you?"

"I was at the party, Eliza. You just didn't see me because the scarecrow kept you so busy," Cassidy said, taking carrots, cucumbers, tomatoes, a bag of salad greens, and a container of black olives from the refrigerator.

"Never mind that," Eliza said, blushing. "What happened with you and James?"

Cassidy took a sharp knife from the drawer and began slicing the tomatoes. "There's nothing to tell, not really," she said.

"Do you take me for a complete fool, Cassidy Chen?" Eliza asked. Cassidy just kept quiet and continued slicing tomatoes. "All right, let's do it this way. I'll ask questions and you give answers. Question number one, did you and James Tang take a walk together into Discovery Park last night?"

Cassidy paused in her slicing and appeared to be thinking. "Sort of, yeah. I took a walk first, and then he ended up joining me."

"So you went into the park first?" Eliza asked. "You just decided to take a walk *by yourself* in the woods? I mean, come on, it was pretty dark."

"The moon was out. I could see okay. Besides, there was a path." She couldn't tell Eliza what had really happened, not yet, anyway. The whole thing just sounded too crazy. "I was just really, really upset when I saw Majesta show up at the party with James as her date. And then she asked me if I was dressed like a shrub. So I went outside to be alone for a while, and then I realized that I just couldn't go back in and have to deal with them again."

"Okay, but what about James?" Eliza asked.

"I'm getting to that," Cassidy said, dropping a handful of chopped tomatoes into a salad bowl. "So I'm in the woods and I hear a sound and there's James. He'd gone outside to cool off. Anyway, I guess he saw that the gate was open and he just walked through down the path. When I saw him, I asked him what time it was and realized I needed to get back. So we both left together."

Eliza didn't say anything for a minute. She studied Cassidy's face as if she might find evidence there of some missing piece to the story. "Hmmm," she said at last. "You two looked, I don't know, kind of . . . well, chummy or something when you came through the gate."

"We *are* friends," Cassidy said. "And apparently that's all we'll ever be now that Majesta's trapped him in her goddess lair."

"I don't think Majesta has James Tang trapped in any kind of lair, Cass," Eliza said, leaning over to pick a baby carrot out of the salad and pop it into her mouth. "But I bet she *wishes* she had him trapped because he was a total hottie in that Zorro costume."

"Yeah, he looked good," Cassidy admitted, feeling a stab of jealousy.

She sliced the cucumbers into thin slivers, just the way she and Eliza liked them. The sound of the stainless steel knife as it sliced through the pale green flesh reminded her of the whirring sound of the thin metallic wings of the snake just before it attacked.

"Ouch!" she cried, dropping the knife and bringing her finger up to her mouth. A couple of drops of blood dripped onto the wood cutting board.

"What happened?" Eliza cried.

Cassidy ran cold water into the sink and held her finger under the flow. "It's just a cut," she said.

"Let's see how bad it is," Eliza said. "You might need stitches."

Cassidy turned off the water and looked at her index finger. There was a faint pink line where she thought she'd been cut. She turned her finger and then looked at her entire hand.

"Where is it?" Eliza asked, turning Cassidy's hand over, examining it from all sides.

"I thought I cut it here," Cassidy said, indicating the almost-invisible mark.

"That can't be it," Eliza said. "That's already healed. You bled, Cassidy—you must have some open wound, a gash, something."

But she didn't. Whatever cut had opened and spilled Cassidy's blood onto the chopping board had healed almost instantly.

🍀 *Chapter Seventeen*

On Wednesday, James was late to Wing Chun for the first time. "*Shifu,* I apologize for my lateness," he said. "I'm truly sorry to interrupt your lesson."

Master Lau nodded and motioned for James to extend his apology to the other students. Cassidy was embarrassed for him, but James seemed to be taking the whole thing in stride. In fact, his apology was almost mocking in tone, but if Master Lau sensed that it was, he didn't say anything. "My fellow students, please accept my apology for interrupting class."

The students nodded in James's direction

and class resumed. Cassidy felt as if Master Lau purposefully drilled them longer than ever on the simplest moves. She lifted her arm to block and then brought it to her chest again. Over and over. Cassidy thought about the way she'd blocked the attack of the snake. She hadn't been able to call it a demon yet, but in her heart she was beginning to wonder if that's what it was.

When Master Lau finally dismissed them, Cassidy changed quickly, hoping to catch James before he left. She pushed open the door to step outside and saw Majesta getting in a car with her sister and taking off. *Great, she's not riding home with James today.* As the car pulled away from the curb, Majesta looked out the window at James standing on the sidewalk, then up the steps at Cassidy. She had an unusual expression on her face. *Is Majesta jealous? Is she mad about James disappearing from the party? Did she know that he was with me that night?*

Not my problem right now, Cassidy said to herself. *I just need to get to the bottom of this.*

"James," she said, unsure of what she planned to say next.

He turned to her and smiled. "Hey, Cass, what's up?"

"I'm just wondering if we could talk about what happened the other night," she said.

James coughed a little self-consciously. "You

were there. You saw what I saw."

"Right," Cassidy admitted. "By the way, thanks again for showing up when—" But she couldn't finish because her cell phone began ringing. A quick glance at caller ID told Cassidy it was her mother. "Sorry, James, I gotta take this. It's my mom."

"No problem," he said.

"Hey, Mom," Cassidy answered, hoping that the conversation would be a quick one and she could get back to James. As she walked down the sidewalk a couple of steps to get better reception, she noticed Luis standing at the bus stop across the street.

"Oh, good, you're out of class. Listen, could you stop by the Happy Bunny on your way home and help me clean up? Robin's had a little emergency at home and had to leave early."

Cassidy felt a sharp jab of disappointment. She'd hoped to have some time to talk to James about the party. "Well . . . okay, sure, Mom. I'll be there in fifteen minutes or so."

She shut the cell phone. "Sorry, James. I have to help my mom out at her preschool. But I need to talk about this. I mean, I can't figure out what really happened."

"Yeah, I guess that would be a good idea. You haven't told anybody else, have you?"

Cassidy shook her head. "Of course not," she said. She took a deep breath. "You?"

"No way," he said emphatically. "Want to meet for coffee or something after school tomorrow? I've gotta be in Fremont to pick up something for my dad."

"Sure," she said. "Tomorrow's good."

"You know Leafy Green's?"

"Next to Art Depot?" Cassidy said.

"Yeah, meet me at Leafy's at four o'clock," James said. "I gotta go. There's my dad."

So, she thought as she walked toward the bus, *I have a sort-of date tomorrow with James Tang! Okay, not really a date . . . But could he be interested in me, too? I mean, he did seem to be flirting with me at the party, and he did come to my rescue. Whatever. I can't think about this now,* she told herself as she boarded the bus. *I've got more important things to figure out.*

As luck would have it, the only empty seat on the bus was next to Luis. Cassidy realized she had approximately fifteen minutes to try to apologize to her friend again.

"Luis, you mind if I sit down?"

"If you have to," he said, not looking up from the martial arts magazine he was reading.

"Luis, I'm really, really sorry. I didn't mean what I said the other day. I'd been kind of sick, and I just sort of snapped and said some really stupid things."

"You got that right," he said.

"Can you forgive me?" she asked.

Luis was silent.

"L Man?" she said, and noticed a quick flicker of a smile. Finally he turned and looked at her.

"I just want you to know that you were completely wrong about Brooke," Luis said. "She *does* like me. She wants me to come to Wilder's next home game."

"Okay, I stand corrected." Cassidy high-fived Luis, and they both smiled. "Go, L Man!" she said.

"Yeah," he said. "I'm not saying there's anything to it, but she likes me. She thinks I'm funny."

"You are funny, Luis," Cassidy said.

"Yeah, sure," he said, sliding the magazine into his messenger bag. "Hey, you need to get home right away? You want to stop off at Jon Paul's?"

"Can't—I've got to help my mom out at the Happy Bunny. One of the assistants had to leave early, and I said I'd help clean up."

"I'm not doing anything," he said. "Want some help?"

"That'd be awesome!" said Cassidy. There was a slight pause, and then Cassidy said softly, "We're good now, right, Luis?"

"Yeah," Luis said. "We're good."

☙☙☙☙☙

During her morning shower the next day,

Cassidy realized that not one mark or bruise remained from her battle with the winged snake. The old bruises had faded to a faint plum, and miraculously there wasn't even a hint that she'd cut her finger with a very sharp knife. *Weird,* Cassidy thought. *How come I healed so quickly?*

Standing in front of her open closet, Cassidy admitted to herself that she was putting a little more thought into what she wore to school that day — even though she had reminded herself over and over that her meeting with James was not a date.

She finally decided to wear the new tangerine wrap sweater her mother had given her for her birthday instead of one of her usual sweatshirts that she loved so much. Checking herself in the mirror before leaving her room, she decided that she felt pretty good about the way she looked. She struck a pose with her chin up, her shoulders back. She wondered if Majesta always felt that kind of confidence. It was a good feeling, she decided, one that she'd like to feel more often.

ↄↄↄↄↄ

"We're moving!" Eliza said in despair, sliding into the seat next to Cassidy, her plaid rain poncho dripping puddles around their feet. Morning assembly hadn't started yet, and the noisy gym thrummed with the sound of students talking and catching up on gossip and homework assignments.

"Come on, Eliza," Cassidy said. "Your mom says that all the time."

"No, this time it's different. She says she's had enough. She showed me all this research she got off the Internet about Phoenix. Phoenix, can you believe it? It's like a giant sandbox! Who wants to live in a sandbox?"

"Eliza, calm down," Cassidy said. "Your mom's always talking about moving and she never does."

"I think she's serious this time. My uncle Lee lives in Phoenix, and he's all excited about us moving. She even had him call me this morning and tell me what a great place it is. How the sun shines practically all the time! I mean, who cares, you know? Who needs the sun to shine all the freaking time? It's not natural!"

"I bet she'll change her mind," Cassidy offered. A sudden clap of thunder rolled over the metal roof of the gym and echoed like a thousand drums.

"I don't think so, Cass. I think this is really it. She says she wants us to be out of here in a couple of months."

The rain pounded the roof, making it impossible to hear Mr. Edwards read the morning announcements. Finally he gave up and dismissed everyone. As she walked to class, Cassidy wondered: *Does Ms. Clifford mean it this time? Will she and Eliza really move?*

❧❧❧❧❧

As she walked to Leafy's through another downpour that afternoon, Cassidy wondered what would happen when she and James compared notes about the attack in the woods. What if she'd let her imagination run wild and nothing all that weird had really happened?

What if James said: *I followed you out there and saw this snake in the woods—I tried to kill it, but then you picked up a stick and killed it yourself.* That certainly made more sense than the unbelievable memories she had of the night in the forest.

❧❧❧❧❧

Leafy Green's was a warm, dry refuge from the watery world outside. Cassidy wiped her wet boots on the mat at the door and dropped her umbrella into the large clay pot with all the others. A quick glance around told her that James wasn't there yet. She decided to go ahead and order. *It's not a date, after all,* she told herself. *It's just two friends having coffee.* Besides, she needed something warm to drink, and the smell of freshly ground coffee beans was irresistible.

Cassidy had gotten her coffee from the counter and was taking a seat at a table in a nook underneath a staircase just as James came in the door. He gave a nod to indicate that he was going to order something.

Cassidy thought about turning off her cell phone. She really didn't want to be interrupted with some minor Happy Bunny emergency, yet it didn't seem right to avoid a call from her mom.

She glanced at her phone and saw *No service* scrolled across the screen. *Thank goodness for the nook at Leafy's,* she thought. She dropped the phone back into the pocket of her backpack as James sat down with his coffee and a small plate of crescent-shaped lemon cookies.

His hair was wet, and he had pushed it back from his face. His intense dark eyes, Cassidy now noticed, were flecked with gold. He wore a faded blue sweatshirt with a Sorrowful Monkeys logo across the front. Vintage, Cassidy knew. The Sorrowful Monkeys had been a popular Seattle grunge band of the eighties.

James looked amazing. *I would be happy just to sit here and look at him. No conversation necessary,* she thought. But he put an end to that when he pushed the plate of lemon cookies across the table to her and said, "So, how did a nice girl like you manage to get in a fight with a wicked demon?"

Chapter Eighteen

"A demon?" Cassidy asked, surprised at his directness and shocked that Mr. Cool himself believed in something as out there as demons.

"You know what they say," said James, breaking off a corner of a cookie and popping it into his mouth. "If it walks like a duck and quacks like a duck . . ."

"Yeah, but come on, a *demon*?" Cassidy asked, feeling compelled to test him. "That's so *supernatural*, you know? Don't you think it was just a snake? There are plenty of snakes in forests. They like the damp, cool—"

"The snake had wings, Cassidy. It was flying," James interrupted, and took a long sip of his coffee. "You saw its eyes. That thing was after you."

"And how do you know so much about demons, James Tang?" she asked.

"My father teaches Chinese literature and mythology at U Dub," he said. "Most kids grow up hearing stories about cute little puppies, curious monkeys, you know, kid stories with happy endings. I grew up in Hong Kong listening to tales about the great Chinese dragon who delivers the rising sun in his jaws each morning and swallows it whole every evening. I've heard all about ghosts, demons, you name it—all the restless, angry spirits roaming the world seeking revenge."

Cassidy was silent for a moment. Was this what she was waiting to hear? Was it possible that James might actually be able to help her figure all this out?

"I'm convinced that there's way more to the world than meets the eye," he continued. "Did you know that some people believe that there's actually some truth to the stories of mythology? That maybe some of these wild creatures that we read about really existed, at least in some form? And maybe still exist . . . who knows?"

James paused and then leaned in closer to Cassidy, who couldn't help but notice that the rich darkness of his eyes was the exact same color as his coffee. "That thing in the woods the other night? That was not your garden-variety snake, Cassidy."

Definitely not, Cassidy thought, *but a demon?*

At tables all around, Cassidy heard the pleasant buzz of friends talking, catching up at the end of the day, planning what they would do that night. There was the sound of spoons clinking against mugs and an occasional call from the counter girl that an order was ready. The absolute normalcy of Leafy Green's Coffee Shop made the conversation that she and James were having seem even more surreal.

Suddenly Cassidy felt her chest tighten. Something had tried to kill her. *Take deep breaths,* she told herself. She'd stepped off the path of logic and reason into some kind of unknown territory—where white snakes could sprout scaly, metallic wings and try to kill you.

But that's where she was, and it was time to find out why.

"Okay, James," she said finally. "You seem to have a pretty open mind, so I'm going to go out on a limb here. There's actually more to the story. A lot more."

And while coffee was brewed, poured, and served, while the buzz of Leafy's danced in the air and jumped from table to table, while the little bell on the door signaled customers coming in and going out again into the drizzly afternoon that quickly turned to evening, Cassidy told James everything.

Two cups of coffee and four lemon cookies later, Cassidy finished her story. She looked into his eyes for his reaction and couldn't help wondering if he had any idea how she felt about him. Outside, the rain had let up and a muted November sunset stained the sky with heavy streaks of pale orange and violet.

"Wow." James shook his head. "So what are you going to do now?"

"I don't know," Cassidy said. "I don't know what any of this even means, but I'm afraid it's not over. I really don't know what to do next."

James was silent for a moment, as if considering what he would do if he were in Cassidy's position.

"My dad has a library at home," he said. "I might be able to find out something about the coins and maybe the winged snake, too."

"James, you saw what happened the other night," Cassidy said. "So I have to ask you this—you know that helping me could be, well, dangerous. Are you sure you want to do this? I mean, why would you even want to?"

"Easy," James said, giving her a reckless smile that she found irresistible. "Just about everything else bores me to tears."

Cassidy and James exchanged e-mail addresses and made plans to meet the following Wednesday after Wing Chun. James told her to bring the coins, her notes about the dreams, and anything else she thought might be helpful. "We'll take the ferry to my house on Bainbridge, and then I'll ask Dad to drive you back."

"Sounds great, James, I really appreciate this," Cassidy said. *Still not a date*, she told herself. *But at least I'll be spending more time with him.*

"Well, I guess I'm out of here," James said. They stood on the rain-slick sidewalk outside Leafy's. "I'm glad you told me about this, Cass."

"Thank you again for showing up when you did," Cassidy said, remembering the feel of her breath as it was being squeezed out of her. She had been ready to give up.

"You're the one who killed it," James said. "You're pretty good with a *nandao*, by the way."

"A what?" Cassidy asked. She remembered James pulling a sword from a scabbard at his waist, but the demon had flicked its powerful tail and knocked it from his hand before he could use it. "You mean the sword? Wasn't that part of your Zorro costume?" she asked.

James laughed. "No, the sword that came with

the costume was plastic and extremely cheap-looking. I borrowed one of my dad's antique broadswords. It's called a *nandao*, and it's about three hundred years old. There's only one other one like it in the world, and that's in a museum in Hong Kong."

"And your dad was okay with this?" Cassidy asked, positive that her parents wouldn't let her out of the house with anything so old and, she was sure, valuable.

"Let's just say he didn't exactly know I borrowed it," James admitted. "It was supposed to be just for show—the scabbard's really cool and the handle looked good. I never expected that we would have to use it, you know?"

Cassidy let this information sink in. She'd killed a demon with a three-hundred-year-old broadsword, practically a *stolen* broadsword. "So, did you tell him anything?"

"No, are you kidding?" James said. "I cleaned it up when I got home and put it back in the case in his library."

"James! You could be in so much trouble," Cassidy said, astonished at his daring. "My parents would kill me!"

"You're lucky I had the real thing with me that night or that demon would have killed both of us."

🌸 Chapter Nineteen

On Thursday night Cassidy and Eliza stood in Cassidy's kitchen waiting for the microwave popcorn to pop.

"He lives on Bainbridge," Cassidy said. "I'm taking the ferry to his house after Wing Chun."

"Yeah, yeah, I get that part," Eliza said. "But is it a date or not?"

"I told you, it's not like that. His dad has all these books on Chinese mythology and martial arts history, and I just figure I might as well learn more about it—I mean, it's my heritage." Cassidy didn't mention that they were also going to research the winged snake that had attacked her in Discovery Park.

"Your story sucks," Eliza said, opening the bag of steaming-hot popcorn and pouring it into a bowl. "That's not why you're going all the way to Bainbridge Island to see James."

Cassidy was beginning to wonder what Eliza knew.

"You're going because James is five kinds of gorgeous *and* he's older *and* you ended up having a great time with him at the party the other night. Besides, it'll drive Majesta nuts."

"That's not why I'm going, Eliza," Cassidy said. "Besides, what's Majesta got to be jealous about? It's not like those two are a couple or anything. They just went to a party together."

"Right," Eliza said. "But they didn't stay at the party together, and she's the one who invited him. I think James pretty much proved that he'd rather spend time with you than Majesta."

Don't I wish! Cassidy thought.

"You know, Clifford," she said, trying to keep a cool, detached tone, "I don't know why I tell you anything. I really am interested in mythology, and James said his dad has this amazing library, and—"

"Oh, save it, Cass," Eliza said, tossing a handful of popcorn into her open mouth. "I'm your friend, remember? I know why you're going to Bainbridge

Island!"

Cassidy felt a pang of remorse. She had never felt the need to keep anything from Eliza before, and now she was piling secrets on top of lies. "Has your mom said anything else about moving?" Cassidy asked.

"Yeah, she's still talking about it. This rain's not helping, you know? She says that's one major reason she wants to move—to get away from all the bad weather."

"It's not like this all the time," Cassidy said.

"Yeah, well, tell her that. She's got a calendar on the fridge, and she marks a big blue raindrop or teardrop or something on every day that it rains."

✺✺✺✺✺

"I'm glad your parents were okay with you coming out to the island with me," James said as he and Cassidy stepped onto the ferry together at Pier 52.

"They know who your dad is," Cassidy explained. "They heard him speak at that lecture series last month."

"Amazing." James shook his head. "I can never believe that people actually attend those lectures. I mean, his students have no choice, but your parents went to a lecture on Chinese mythology for *fun*?"

"Yeah, small world," she said. She held on to the wooden railing of the ferry's lower deck. The sky was a funny grayish green, and the air seemed charged. Another storm was brewing to the west, clouds building into an ominous mass of fury and flood.

"I guess we'll have to sit inside," James said. "I don't think this rain's ever going to stop. But then again, this is Seattle, right?"

"Yeah, but this is, like, record breaking or something," Cassidy said.

They found a table on the top deck near the café. To Cassidy's surprise, James didn't bring up the reason they were going to his house. Instead he talked a little about his life in San Francisco before they moved to Seattle.

"How old were you when you left Hong Kong?" Cassidy asked.

"Eight," he said. "Same year my mother died."

"I'm sorry about your mother," Cassidy said. "I've never lost anyone close to me."

"Not even a grandparent?" James asked.

"My grandparents died before I was born," she told him. "I never got to know any of them."

⌬⌬⌬⌬⌬

James's father was a tall man in his early fifties. He had dark hair that was a little long, but it didn't look intentionally long, like James's. It looked as if he had simply forgotten to schedule a haircut in a while. He wore a dark tweed jacket over a pair of tan khakis. A couple of pens and a small spiral notebook stuck out of his right jacket pocket. Cassidy could see a family resemblance, but there was a rumpled, tired look about Professor Tang.

"Cassidy," he said after shaking her hand in the ferry parking lot, "so good to meet you. I enjoyed talking with your father on the phone. I hope I didn't bore them to death at the community lecture last month. I had been told to keep it peppy, but that's kind of hard to do when you're speaking on the influence of the global egg theory on Chinese creation myths."

"Actually, they said they enjoyed it very much," Cassidy told him.

"Well, you're very kind," Mr. Tang said, opening the door to his car and ushering her in. "Maybe we can get to the house before the next storm. I think I may have to trade in this automobile for a boat if the rain keeps up."

As if on cue, a cloud opened and rain came down in blowing gusts. "Did you know that it was believed that some of the worst flooding occurred when a mortal had upset a dragon?" the professor said. "In some Chinese villages there are still temples dedicated to the local Dragon King. Especially those villages built near rivers or other bodies of water. Local officials would lead the community to the temple, where sacrifices were made to appease the angry dragon."

"What was sacrificed?" Cassidy asked, wondering if she really wanted to know.

"Well, that would depend on the severity of the flood. It might be as simple as an offering of food or as serious as a human life—especially if the officials believed they had found the mortal who had angered the dragon in the first place."

"That's terrible," Cassidy said. "But interesting." She remembered James saying he'd grown up with stories like these. It was no wonder that he had been so open to Cassidy's story about the coins and the dreams, not to mention what he'd seen with his own eyes in the forest.

"So, Cassidy," James said from the backseat, "you think we can find out who angered the dragon this time? I'm sick of this constant rain—it's time for some sacrifice."

James's father began to laugh. "One of my colleagues believes it's those darn Seahawks and their awful losing streak. He says it's time to sacrifice the coach!"

☙☙☙☙☙

The Tangs' house was on a large wooded lot. It was sprawling, beautiful, and austere. There was none of the warmth that Cassidy felt in her own home, with her mother's Happy Bunny craft supplies in disarray around the rooms or the sound of her father's favorite country-western music on the stereo. The rooms were sparsely furnished, with an interesting mix of highly polished, severe contemporary pieces and large, forbidding Chinese antiques. *Where's Mr. Tang's comfortable recliner? Where are the pillows and cushions and soft rugs?* Cassidy thought.

Mr. Tang hung Cassidy's coat on a curved panel of wrought-iron hooks near the door. "Would you like something to eat, Cassidy, something to drink?"

"I'm fine," she said. "Thanks anyway."

"Very well," he said. "James, why don't you show Cassidy to the library?"

෨෨෨෨෨

Professor Tang's library was lined with floor-to-ceiling bookshelves. James went over to a long table near the back of the room and switched on a brass lamp that cast a circular pool of light onto the dark wood. Against one wall was a large glass case containing a number of weapons. Cassidy recognized the three-hundred-year-old *nandao* she had used to kill the winged snake.

"You know," she said slowly, "when I used that blade on the snake, it was so strange. I mean, I've never used a knife to hurt—or kill—anything before. But the moment I picked up the *nandao*, it felt exactly right in my hands."

James looked at her, his dark eyes unreadable. "Have you practiced with weapons before?"

"No. Not even a little."

He shrugged. "Well, then you must have some kind of natural ability for it." He went over to one of the bookshelves and removed a large book bound in dark brown leather. "I got kind of a head start on the research," he explained. "I found something in one of Dad's books that may be helpful." He opened the book gently, taking care as he turned thin pages of yellowed, brittle paper.

"There," he said, pointing to a small boxed sketch. "Is that our demon?"

She looked at it closely. "Well, it's a snake with wings," she said. "So, I guess that could be it."

"Let's see the coins," James said. "And if we hear Dad coming, hide them. Believe me, if he finds out about any of this, he'll want to research it to death. He'll get studies done and—"

"Then let's definitely keep them hidden," Cassidy agreed. "I don't want to get anybody else involved in this—not yet, anyway."

Cassidy took the wooden box from her backpack and opened it, removing the five coins and the note. James took a large magnifying glass from a silver tray in the middle of the table and examined the coins front and back.

"I'd say this drawing is a pretty good match," James said. "What do you think?"

"Yeah, but what does it mean?" Cassidy asked, noting that the text in the caption below the sketch was written entirely in Chinese. "I hope you can read it."

"I can't, but I asked Dad to translate a little for me the other day. Apparently a winged snake represents poison sickness. To be cursed by this type of demon means that you gradually get sicker and sicker until you're weak and helpless. You become the victim of accidents and bad luck. There's a myth about a man who was cursed by the winged snake," James went on. "Three months later he begged to be killed because he just couldn't take it any longer."

Cassidy shuddered, understanding how the man must have felt.

She picked up the coin showing the winged snake with exposed fangs. "You think that somehow the snake could have been poisoning me for a while? Like since my birthday?"

"Could be," James said. "In the myths the curse was sort of the demon's first line of attack, you know? If the curse itself didn't kill you—poisoning you and causing freak accidents—then you'd at least be too weak to fight when the demon finally attacked."

Cassidy remembered Patrick Healy's diagnosis. *He was right. I was cursed.*

"My dad also said that it was the custom of warriors hundreds of years ago to have a gold coin made whenever they defeated some enemy that had been really powerful. They would engrave some symbol of the enemy's power onto the coin."

"Yeah, I read something about that on the Internet."

"There was a superstition that the coins actually trapped the spirit of the enemy and that if it was ever released, it would seek revenge. But here's the weird part. He also said that if the demon was defeated, then the coin could transfer some power or gift to whoever killed it."

"What kind of gift?" she asked.

"I don't know," James said. "I guess some kind of supernatural gift or whatever."

Cassidy thought about the day she'd cut her finger and it had healed immediately. It was as if it hadn't even happened. *Was that some kind of gift or power? But of what? Of healing quickly?*

While James examined the other coins through the magnifying glass, Cassidy walked over to the long windows and looked out across the lawn. The dark evergreens bent from the wind that shrieked around the corners of the house, and the rain came down in silvery blinding sheets.

"Found something," James called. He had three other books spread out on the table. "We're lucky — this one's in English."

Cassidy returned to the table, where James had placed one of the coins next to a drawing. "A wave demon?" Cassidy asked, reading the caption.

"Yeah," James said. "It's the symbol of Chuan Lei, who is actually a ghost known for causing floods. He's also called a plague ghost."

"Plague ghost?" Cassidy asked, fingering the outline of the wave on the gold coin. "Floods?"

"Yeah, we're talking major, ancient ghost. Maybe it'll make more sense if I just read it," James said. He pulled the lamp in closer and read:

"In Chinese mythology, the plague ghost of Chuan Lei can be as small as a drop of water or as large as the ocean. According to a southern Chinese legend, Chuan Lei was once a mortal himself who was almost as powerful as a dragon, but he became greedy and used his strength for evil purposes. He flooded villages and drowned thousands in order to take their land.

"One legend claims that he boasted that no one could stop him, not even the renowned women fighters Ng Mui and Wing Chun. Chuan Lei traveled a great distance to their village to prove that he was the most powerful fighter in all of China.

"Even before Chuan Lei arrived, the rain began.

When he reached the river at the edge of the village, it was already swollen with dark water that threatened to spill over the banks. Wing Chun waited for Chuan Lei on the opposite bank as patient as a crane waiting at the edge of the water. Chuan Lei laughed at her size, and Wing Chun surprised him by quickly crossing the river on top of the crests of angry waves. The battle was fierce but brief. Wing Chun destroyed Chuan Lei, and the flood stopped immediately."

"Wing Chun?" Cassidy asked. "I didn't know it was named after a woman."

"Yeah," James said. "I had a *shifu* in San Francisco who drilled us constantly on the animal stances and attacks that were developed by those two women. He said that an animal knows how to find the weakness in its enemy. Imagine, Wing Chun taking on the powerful Chuan Lei—and she defeats him!"

"So, she somehow found his weakness, and I'm guessing she had a coin made, right?" Cassidy asked. "This coin?"

"Maybe—I don't know. It sure looks like the one in the drawing."

Cassidy placed the wave coin next to the sketch in the book. It was a match, even down to the hollow eyes that floated in the sky just above the horizon of waves.

"Wait a minute," Cassidy said, looking away from the book and straight at James. "I have a coin with a snake on it and I was attacked by a snake demon. So now I have a coin that shows a wave—what does it mean, James? That a dead person, or maybe his *ghost*, is going to come after me?"

James flipped the coin over and pointed to the two slightly raised marks on the back. "The snake demon coin is marked with one stroke. This one has two. I don't know if that has anything to do with order or not."

The other three coins lay on the table. They were marked three, four, and five, but Cassidy couldn't think about that now—didn't want to think about it.

"James, this is crazy," Cassidy said. "Why are these things happening? The coins, the demons—this kind of stuff isn't supposed to happen in real life."

"I don't know," he admitted. "But whatever it is seems to be connected to your dreams, and I bet that's where you'll find the answer. You told me that a woman in your dream said this is your destiny."

"That was just a dream, James. A *dream*!"

"Could be a visitation—maybe from an ancestor. Some people believe that we're given guidance by our ancestors and that the messages come to us in dream form."

Cassidy massaged her temples. "This is too much," she said. "I think I just reached my limit on how much supernatural hoo-ha I can take in one evening. I mean, an angry ghost who brings floods?"

"Yeah, and a flying white snake whose curse nearly killed you even before you fought it," James reminded her. "Somehow I don't think being skeptical is going to be too helpful here."

"Oh, really? Well, then, what do you find most helpful when you're fighting ghosts?"

James smiled. Then he moved the book, touching the back of her wrist lightly, and Cassidy felt a little thrill go through her. The door to the library opened then, and Professor Tang walked in. Cassidy noticed that James quickly placed the book over the coins.

"Sorry to interrupt your studies," Professor Tang said. "But there is a weather warning of possible flooding on some of the roads. I'm afraid I should return you to your home, Cassidy, before it gets any worse."

Chapter Twenty

The drive back to the ferry was an almost silent one except for the tempest raging outside. Professor Tang was a careful driver and was forced to inch along due to the near-zero visibility beyond the windshield of his car. From time to time a blinding flash of jagged lightning split the dark sky followed by a deafening explosion of thunder that sounded as if the entire world were being ripped in half.

As Professor Tang drove off the ferry ramp onto the drenched Seattle streets, Cassidy's cell phone began to ring. "Thank goodness, Cassidy," her mother said. "I've been trying to call for an hour, but there was no service. A lot of the streets are flooding. I hope you're on the way home."

"Yeah, Mom," Cassidy said. "We're about fifteen minutes away." She closed the phone. "Sorry we have to rush," she said to Professor Tang and James.

"Your mother would naturally be worried," Professor Tang said. "A good mother always worries."

Cassidy detected a note of sadness in his voice. Was he thinking about James's mother? James had said they left Hong Kong right after his mother died. *Were they running from grief—from sadness? Is it possible to just run away from something bad?* Cassidy thought about the coins that had been given to her. Could she simply run from them? Forget about them? *Could I go back to the normal life of a fourteen-year-old girl who doesn't have to think about things like demons and ghosts?*

She could see the outline of both her parents standing in the front window of her house when Professor Tang pulled into the driveway.

"They're waiting for you," he said, smiling at her. "Please come back anytime, Cassidy; maybe when the weather is better."

"Thank you, Professor," she said. "Thanks,

James, for all the, uh"—Cassidy stumbled for a second—"information." *Did his father notice the pause?* "Would you like to come in?" she said, knowing that was what her parents would expect her to ask.

"We should get back to the island before they close the ferries," Professor Tang said. "Perhaps another time."

"See you, Cass," James said from the backseat. "I'll e-mail you."

James and his father waited in the driveway with the lights on as Cassidy ran through the driving rain to the covered front stoop.

ⓢⓢⓢⓢⓢ

Inside, Cassidy's mother had a pot of chicken soup bubbling on the stove. The kitchen was fragrant with the smell of rosemary. Cassidy changed out of her wet clothes into some warm sweats before joining her parents for dinner. Monty lay across her feet under the table. The events of the last few hours seemed a million miles away in the peaceful comfort of her home.

Yet outside, the storm raged, and in the family room a television weather reporter delivered dire predictions about the future of Seattle if the weather didn't improve soon.

"I'm sorry you had to cut your visit short, Cassidy," Wendy said as she passed a plate of crusty bread to Simon. "But this weather . . . it's actually getting dangerous out there. The power's out in parts of the city."

"Maybe you'll have a chance to go back to Bainbridge when the weather improves," her father said. "Did you get a chance to look at any of Professor Tang's books?"

The chicken soup warmed Cassidy and seemed the perfect thing to take the damp chill from her bones. She wanted to talk to her parents about what was going on. It was becoming too overwhelming to keep it all to herself.

"Yeah, Dad," Cassidy said, stirring the fragrant soup in her bowl. "Actually, James was helping me find out about the coins. You know, the ones I got for my birthday."

Her father looked over at her mother, as if to ask, *Did you know about this?* "So, did you find out anything interesting?" he asked.

"Well, we found sketches of two of them," Cassidy said. "One is a winged snake and another represents something called a plague ghost. They were made to commemorate battles, like tokens to mark the defeat of an enemy."

"That *is* interesting," her father said. "Although it still doesn't answer the question of why the coins were given to you."

"I know," Cassidy said, thinking about the

strange old man who showed up on her fourteenth birthday and handed her the box of coins without saying a word. If only she could ask *him* that question.

⊘⊘⊘⊘⊘

Before going to bed, Cassidy signed on to check her e-mail. Luis had sent her a video of a monkey dancing hip-hop, which was a good sign and meant that he had truly forgiven her for what she'd said. There were also two e-mails from Eliza. The first e-mail was just one word: *Well?* Which meant that Eliza wanted to know how the *date* with James Tang went. The second e-mail was also from Eliza—a rambling, rather frantic-sounding paragraph saying that a packet of information from a real estate office in Phoenix had arrived in the mail and she was thinking about burning it before her mother got home.

Cassidy clicked on Reply and started to write some words of comfort to Eliza, but she couldn't think of anything to say. *I'm scared,* Cassidy realized.

Earlier in the semester, a guidance counselor spoke at morning assembly about the stresses that teens go through. She told the students about a teen chat room that was monitored by trained counselors twenty-four hours a day. Cassidy typed in the address and registered with the screen name Mingmei. It felt odd typing the name, but she didn't want anyone she

177

knew to recognize her name or even her initials.

The room opened, and Cassidy skimmed through some of the problems being discussed. A student identified as JerLang5 wrote that he was failing almost every class because it was just too hard to keep up. He didn't know what to do, and he just kept getting more and more behind. Someone else wrote that her boyfriend just broke up with her and she couldn't stop crying.

Cassidy wondered what would happen if she wrote: *I've already had to fight what appears to have been a snake demon and now I find out that in all likelihood a plague ghost wants me dead. By the way, it's the very same plague ghost that's caused all the flooding these last few days. There are three more demons to go, and I just don't think I can take this anymore. What should I do?*

She'd probably be kicked out of the chat room for violating the terms of service, that's what. The terms of agreement spelled out that the room was for serious discussion of teenage problems only. Her problem was nothing like the ones being discussed. Cassidy suddenly felt very lost and alone. She remembered the woman in her dream saying that being a warrior was a lonely fate. Was there nowhere she could go for help? She thought of James, the only person who really knew what she was facing.

I'll e-mail him, she decided. She opened the screen and typed in his e-mail address. In the subject area she wrote **Help.** Then she wrote:

 J.
 Hey, how goes it? Still raining here. Not a good sign. Been thinking about what you said. I don't know what's true or real anymore. Okay, the snake demon was real enough. I'm still trying to wrap my mind around the rest of it.

 I have a terrible feeling you were right—about everything, even the plague ghost. And what really scares me is I don't know if I can stop whatever's coming next. What if it was just luck that I was able to kill the snake demon before it killed me? I just want to say enough already and make it all be over, but I don't know how. What am I supposed to do?
 C.

 Cassidy hit Send and then went back to Eliza's e-mail. She told her not to worry about a move to Phoenix, that it would never happen.
 An instant message box popped up on her screen. It was from James.

Tang05J: got your e-mail. don't know what to tell you, but if I were

fighting an angry ghost, I think I'd
ask for help from my ancestors like
those ladies from your dream—maybe
they all know each other from a
previous life or something

WCHUNGRL: help from ancestors?
meaning???

Tang05J: make a shrine, light
candles, burn incense

WCHUNGRL: that's it??? that's your
help???

Tang05J: couldn't hurt

Some help, Cassidy was thinking as she crawled
into bed and pulled Monty over to her pillow. *Make a
shrine to my ancestors? I don't even know who my ancestors
are. Besides, how is that supposed to help?*

Outside, the wind continued to howl. *It's howling
like a banshee,* her mother had said at dinner as they sat
in the warm dining room eating chicken soup.

"A banshee?" Cassidy had said. "What's that?"

"Well, I don't know exactly," Wendy admitted,
spoon poised on its way to her mouth. "It's something
I remember my grandmother saying when I was a little

girl. I think it means a screaming woman or something like that. Do you know, Simon?"

"Nope, I've heard the saying, but I've never thought about what it means," he had answered.

Cassidy decided she wanted to know — anything to get her mind off her problems. She moved Monty aside as gently as possible and took the dictionary from a bookshelf next to her desk.

She thumbed through until she found it:

banshee (ban'shē) **n.** in Irish and Scottish folktales, a female spirit who is supposed to wail or shriek as a sign that someone in a family is about to die

Terrific, she thought, slamming the dictionary shut. *Just what I needed to read.* She crawled back into bed, cradling Monty to her neck, and then pulled the covers over her head.

ᘯᘯᘯᘯᘯ

Later that night Cassidy awoke when she heard a slapping sound at her window and then felt a spray of water on her face. *Is my window up?* Cassidy got out of bed and ran across the damp floor to the open window, her pale curtains drenched from the rain. *But there's no way I would have left it open.* Her heart raced from the unexpected awakening.

She pushed the window down securely and then latched it. Looking out through the darkness, she could see the silhouette of evergreens swaying and bent from the howling gusts. *Maybe the wind pushed it open.* But even as she thought it, she realized that the wind couldn't have pushed the window up. *Besides, I'm sure it was locked!*

The rain blew harder now, slapping at her window like a flattened hand intent on breaking through the glass. She instinctively took a step back, and as she did, a gnarled, wet hand, as large as five human ones, appeared at her window. The drenched hand pressed against the glass, and she could see dark spidery lines crisscrossing the huge, greenish gray palm.

Chapter Twenty-One

Cassidy screamed but was unable to move or look away from the watery hand outside her window. Moments later the door to her room was flung open and her mother rushed toward her, followed closely by her dad.

"What's wrong, Cass?" her mother said.

Cassidy pointed toward the window. "I saw a hand. It was trying to . . . to get in!"

"You're just having a bad dream, sweetheart," Wendy told her.

Her father walked over to the window and

peered out. "Leaves," he said. "See, these leaves have blown against the window—that's what you were seeing."

"It looked just like a hand—a big hand with long fingers—and it was pushing on the glass!"

"Dreams can seem very real," her mother said soothingly. "But it was just a dream—there's no hand or anything out there trying to get in, except maybe the rain."

"That's why I woke up," Cassidy told them. "I felt rain on my face, and when I got up, I saw that my window was open."

"Had you opened it earlier?" Simon asked her.

"No, Dad," Cassidy told him. "It's cold outside. There's no way I would have opened it."

"Maybe in your sleep, then," her mother suggested. "You must have opened it in your sleep, and then when you felt the rain, it scared you and you thought you saw something—but look, honey, nothing's there."

Wendy guided Cassidy to the window so that she could see for herself that nothing was out there except another raging storm and several dark leaves pressed against the windowpanes.

Just leaves, Cassidy told herself after her parents left her room. As she tried to go back to sleep, she imagined the dark leaves against the glass with their delicate veins visible to her from the inside. But all she could see was the grotesque hand, its palm lined, its long fingers pressed against the window, ready to break through.

❦❦❦❦❦

The first thing Cassidy did when she woke up the next morning was look out the window. No nightmarish hand now, only another gray morning of heavy rain and endless wind. Downstairs, her parents were drinking coffee in front of the television, watching round-the-clock weather coverage. The weather map of the United States showed a heavy purple blob over the entire Seattle area. Within the purple were splotches of orange and red, indicating even more severe thunderstorms in those areas.

"Morning, Cass," Wendy said, looking up from her coffee. "You feeling better today? No more scary dreams?"

"No, that was the only one, but it sure seemed real," Cassidy said. "Sorry about waking you up."

A weather warning beeped, and the television ran a notice along the bottom of the screen. "Well, now, the ferries have stopped running," her father said. "No ferry service until further notice."

"Has school been canceled?" Cassidy asked hopefully.

"No, not yours, anyway," Simon told her. "All

of Bainbridge and Vashon are closed. The power is out on both islands. Part of downtown Seattle, too."

"So many streets are flooded that a lot of the buses can't get through," Wendy added. "Most of the houseboat families have started heading south, too. These weather guys have no clue when the rain's going to stop."

Cassidy thought about the wave coin. *What am I supposed to do? Just sit here and watch my entire city flood?* But her more logical and reasonable self stepped forward and said, *Don't be silly, Cassidy, weather's a natural phenomenon. You have nothing to do with this.*

"I better get out of here," Simon said. "It's going to take longer to get to work this morning. I'm going to have to take a detour."

"Be careful," Wendy told him. "And call me when you get there."

"Sure, dear," he said, kissing her on top of her head. "Stay dry, Cassidy. Sugar melts in the rain, you know."

"Oh, Dad, that's so corny," Cassidy said with a laugh.

"You should get ready, Cass," her mother said, watching Simon pull out of the garage, windshield wipers slapping the rain at full force. "If we get to school early, maybe I can drop you closer to the front door and you won't get soaked. If you want, call Eliza, too."

"Sure, Mom," Cassidy said. "You think the football game will be called off again?"

Wendy shook her head. It had become a joke now. Since the beginning of the Cleary Street Warriors' season, out of four scheduled games, the team had played only once due to all the rain.

"Actually, *all* after-school activities have been called off," Wendy told her. "It's a good thing, too, because I'm going to need you at the Happy Bunny later."

"Today?" Cassidy asked. She'd been hoping to avoid spending an afternoon with confined preschoolers who couldn't go outside to run off their energy. Rainy days at the Happy Bunny called for a special kind of patience that Cassidy wasn't sure she had right now.

"I'm afraid so," Wendy said. "Since the ferries aren't running, June can't make it in from Vashon and Carol can't get here from Bainbridge."

"All right, Mom, let me call Eliza and see if she can help, too," Cassidy said. *This is getting beyond ridiculous,* she was thinking as she hit speed dial to call Eliza. *The world outside is washing away, it may be my fault, and I'm going to be stuck making paper plate turkeys all afternoon!*

☙ ☙ ☙ ☙ ☙

The school day was interminably long. Several of Cassidy's classes were taught by substitutes because the teachers couldn't make it in due to the flooding. At lunch Luis joined Cassidy and Eliza at a table near the window, where they watched the day turn into another ruined watercolor.

"Hey, did you hear about Master Lau's?" Luis asked, placing his lunch tray on the table. "Flooded out. Water in the street flowed into the studio and ruined the wood floors and a bunch of equipment. His office is damaged, too. A lot of his books got wet."

"That's terrible!" Cassidy said, remembering the low shelves in Master Lau's office, filled with books on martial arts.

"Yeah, he's closed for at least two weeks," Luis said. "This rain is crazy, you know, and it's making people crazy, too."

"What do you mean, it's making people crazy?" Eliza asked. "It's just rain."

"My mom's an emergency room nurse," Luis said. "She says they're getting all kinds of weird injuries and strange behavior in the ER. Stuff they don't usually see."

"You're full of it, Luis," Eliza said. "How could people start acting different or weird just because of the weather? That makes zero sense, and you know it."

And what would Eliza say about the plague ghost?

Cassidy thought. *That makes zero sense, too, but I know what happened—correction, what's STILL happening.*

There was nobody she could really talk to about this—well, nobody except James. And he was stuck on Bainbridge, where both the electrical power and all phone lines were now out.

As the dark torrent continued and her two best friends argued about whether or not the rain could make people do crazy things, Cassidy realized she'd never felt so alone.

ଚ\ଚ\ଚ\ଚ\ଚ

Soaked to the skin, Cassidy and Eliza finally made it to the Happy Bunny at the end of the school day. One look at her mother and Cassidy could see that she was in desperate need of a break. Robin, her afternoon assistant, had called to say that her street was flooded and she couldn't make it in.

"Go in the back and have some coffee or something," Cassidy said. "Eliza and I can take care of the kids for a while. At least there aren't so many of them today."

"Just twelve," her mother said. "Fourteen couldn't make it in. Or maybe they were just smart and stayed home."

"I see Sebastian's here today," Cassidy said, and smiled at her mother.

"Yeah, neither rain nor hail nor snow nor dark of night stops the Sebastians of the world."

Cassidy heard a whimper at her feet. A small puppy, storm gray in color, looked up at her from a green towel near the door. "Are you taking in dogs now, too, Mom?"

"Can you believe it? This puppy showed up about an hour ago, scratching at the door, crying—completely soaked! What was I going to do? We brought him inside and dried him off. I made a little bed for him by the door and told him to stay there."

"No collar or anything?" Eliza asked.

"No—I'm hoping his owner will miss him and start asking around. For now we can at least keep him dry. I told the kids that the puppy's tired and they should leave him alone. But of course, they all want to pick him up and play with him."

"You look completely beat, Mom," Cassidy said. "Go take a break."

"Yeah, this is totally manageable, Mrs. Chen," Eliza said, picking up a construction paper hand that was decorated like a turkey. "Cassidy and I will finish the crafts with the kids, and then we'll read them a story or something."

"You girls are great," Wendy said, visibly exhausted. "Call me if the kids get out of hand. They've been kind of nervous and edgy all day—the storms, the rain. Parent pickup doesn't start until around five thirty, so we've got a ways to go."

Wendy disappeared around the corner and then stuck her head back around. "Oh yeah, the latch on the front door has been kind of sticking, and if there's a gust of wind, it tends to blow open. Scares the kids to death."

"Can't we just lock it?" Eliza asked.

"No, fire code violation—just keep an eye on it," she said. "It may not happen again."

Cassidy took six of the kids to one table and Eliza took the other six and they started tracing around each child's hand with a crayon on a piece of brown construction paper. There was a basket of yellow and orange feathers in the middle of each table, along with several jars of paste.

"That tickles," four-year-old Sebastian said as Cassidy traced in between his chubby fingers.

"We're almost through," Cassidy said, trying to hold his wiggling little hand in place. "Hold still . . . There, all done!"

"Funny turkey," he said. "Now a puppy."

"Maybe later, Sebastian. Why don't you cut out your turkey first?" Cassidy asked. "Lily's cutting out her turkey. See?" Across the table, four-year-old Lily was using a pair of safety scissors to carefully snip around each small finger of her construction paper turkey.

"Help me!" cried another small boy with tears

in his eyes. "I cut off my turkey's head!"

"Oh, no problem," Cassidy said, getting up from her seat and putting her arm around the crying boy. "We can fix him all up."

Cassidy glanced across the room at Eliza, who was having difficulties with the six children at her table. In front of one little girl was a mound of brown paper confetti, growing larger as she continued to cut what should have been a turkey into shreds.

"That's a nice turkey, Chris," Cassidy commented to a small boy next to her wearing glasses. "You want to paste your feathers on now?" She reached across the table and moved the basket of feathers closer and gave three-year-old Chris his own jar of paste.

Looking back across the table, she noticed that Sebastian had abandoned his seat. The brown paper with his chubby hand outline was untouched at his place.

"Sebastian?" Cassidy said, looking toward the door that led to the restrooms. But Lily pointed toward the front door, where Sebastian was headed with his arms outstretched to hold the little dog.

"Puppy! Puppy!" he squealed. The gray puppy was already on his feet, tail wagging, urging Sebastian closer.

"We can't play with the puppy now, Sebastian. He needs to rest," Cassidy said, walking around the art table to catch up with him. She hoped that he wouldn't throw a tantrum and demand to play with the little dog.

Just before she reached him, a sudden gust of wind blew the door wide open. Construction paper turkeys and colorful orange and yellow feathers flew off the tables and sailed through the room. A cold rain sprayed Cassidy, and without thinking, she reached up to shield her eyes.

"Pup-eeeeeeee!" she heard Sebastian cry, his little voice pulled thin and high by the wind that howled like a siren. Cassidy moved toward him, but he was already out the door.

"Sebastian!" Cassidy shrieked. "Come back here!"

Cassidy couldn't believe how fast Sebastian ran. She took off after him, wiping the rain out of her eyes to see, but her wet clothes slowed her down.

Cassidy's heart dropped when she saw that Sebastian had reached the drawbridge at the end of the street. She forced herself to run faster and caught him just as he reached the midpoint of the bridge. She lifted him into her arms. "Puppy," he said, trying to wriggle free.

"No, Sebastian," Cassidy said. "We've got to get back." The footing was slippery, and she almost fell as the orange-and-blue girders seemed to shift beneath her feet. To her horror, she realized that the drawbridge had begun its ascent. *They never open the bridge when someone's on it. This isn't normal.*

Still holding Sebastian, Cassidy peered down at the narrow booth where the bridge operator always stood. "Stop the bridge!" she screamed. "There are people up here!"

"No one in there," Sebastian told her, and she realized he was right. The booth was empty.

Cassidy felt herself panicking. The bridge lurched, knocking her to her knees, and then stopped abruptly.

The entire structure seemed to jerk, and then it began lowering, slowly at first and then faster and faster. Cassidy held Sebastian with one arm and a steel cable with the other. The bridge groaned, gears grinding as their section slammed down and tried to lock into place. *Where's the rest of the bridge?* Cassidy looked up and saw the other half still pointing skyward. *Something's definitely wrong. We've got to get out of here!* Cassidy got to her feet, holding Sebastian tightly, and looked back toward the bank. *Can we make it? If we start running now, can we get to the street?*

But before she could make the decision to run, a large evergreen, bent from the wind, was yanked from the nearby bank and toppled onto the end of the bridge. Splintered wood and dark tangled branches blocked their only way out like a solid wall.

"See the puppy!" Sebastian cried. "Get the puppy, Cassidy, get him!"

Cassidy looked to where he pointed and saw the furious white froth of Lake Washington below. The mist curled as it rose, and Cassidy saw the shape of the gray puppy begin to shift and change on the roiling surface of the water.

It's not a puppy at all, she realized with horror. A hideous bearded face appeared. His skin was mucus green, and his hair moved and swirled around his head in a sickening, continuous motion. She couldn't stop looking at the laughing face in the waters below. The creature's eyes were large and empty of all color. *So this is what lured Sebastian out of the preschool!*

"Monster!" Sebastian screamed, and started crying. He held Cassidy tightly around the neck.

"Sebastian, just hold on, okay? Don't let go."

She looked for a way out. A walkway that workers had been using for maintenance extended out from the edge of the lake several yards just under the main bridge. *How far down is it? Five feet? More? Could we make it? It's so narrow—should I risk it?*

Cassidy looked around, trying to find any other way back to safety. The rain came down hard, pushed by billowing gusts that threatened to rip her hand from the cable she was holding on to. *He's trying to blow us both into the water!* She felt Sebastian being pulled from her and his little arms tightening around her neck in fear. His cries were lost in the wind.

I have to do it. I have to get to the walkway. She knew

that if she didn't act soon, the plague ghost would yank them both off the bridge and into the furious waters of the lake.

"It's not really a monster, Sebastian, it's just the water, okay?" Cassidy knew she was only saying this to try and calm the little boy. There was no denying whether or not this was the plague ghost anymore. As if he'd read her mind, the creature in the water below began to laugh. His voice was as hollow and empty as an echo chamber, and it chilled her with its hatred.

"Give me the boy," he said. "Give me the boy and I'll leave the city."

James was right, she realized with a sickening feeling. *He wants a sacrifice!*

Without answering, Cassidy began moving closer to the edge. She looked down at the narrow walkway. There was no way they could both drop down to the ledge at the same time—it was too risky. *But what if I lower Sebastian onto it?*

"Whatever you're thinking of trying, it's no use." The plague ghost laughed again. "I'll take you, anyway, but if you want to stop the floods, release the boy to the water."

"Sebastian, listen to me," Cassidy whispered into his ear. "See that little bridge down there? I'm going to hold both your hands and lower you onto it. Then I want you to run to the Happy Bunny as fast as you can. Can you run fast?"

"Yes." Sebastian's voice was small, and Cassidy prayed she was doing the right thing.

"Remember, run back to the Happy Bunny," Cassidy said, inching under the steel cable. She held Sebastian by his small wrists and then took a deep breath before lowering him. For a split second she could see his legs dangle, and she wondered if she had miscalculated the distance. But then she saw one foot make contact and then the other. She released his wrists, and to her relief, she saw him pause for a moment and then begin running down the walkway toward the shore. He stopped once more to look back. She could barely see him now through the rain that blew in heavy gusts.

"No, Sebastian! Keep running! I'll be there soon!"

The water below her churned. The plague ghost was furious, Cassidy realized. *I have to get to the ledge.* Holding on to the steel cable, she edged her legs off the bridge. She flexed her foot to feel for the walkway. *Where is it?* She turned her head to look down and was horrified to see the wooden supports of the walkway snap in half as if they were made of toothpicks. The entire structure folded and then crashed into the water below. Cassidy prayed that Sebastian had made it across.

Stinging water shot out of the lake and turned into a curling hand with long fingers that pulled at

Cassidy as she dangled now from the steel cable. She held on with a strength that surprised her.

"You've just doomed your city," the plague ghost bellowed. "How can you be so stupid?"

An enormous white hand of watery mist reached up again and swatted at Cassidy as if she were a fly. This time she felt her hands slip from the cable. Instinct told her to fill her lungs with air as she began the dizzying fall into the violent swirl of water where the plague ghost waited for her.

❀ Chapter Twenty-Two

Cassidy hit the churning water feet first and shot down through its depths like a torpedo. At a point just before hitting the silty lake bed, she kicked and found herself moving up toward the dim lights that seemed a million miles away. *Don't panic,* she told herself. *Just keep swimming.* She struggled through the gray-green water to reach the surface and the promise of air.

How long had she been underwater? She needed oxygen. She had to surface soon to take another breath. Kicking, she realized that her legs were caught in something. She twisted her body and was horrified to see that the plague ghost had wrapped ropy tendrils of mud-colored water around her feet. She was being pulled down to the bottom of the lake.

It's just water, she told herself, and continued to kick furiously. *The water can't hold me!* And with another kick, her feet broke free and she surfaced, gulping the air as it burned her throat. But the battle was far from over. Now the plague ghost was circling furiously, creating a whirlpool in the water below the bridge. Cassidy felt herself being sucked into the vortex. She tried to resist by swimming against the swirling water, but it was impossible to fight the incredible force created by the powerful inverted cone.

There was no time to think of a plan as she was pulled deeper into the spinning whirl. James's only advice had been to call on her ancestors, and she wondered how that could help her now. But as he had written in his e-mail, it certainly couldn't hurt. "Ancestors," she called out loud. "Please, I need your help!" She wondered if that was enough. How was she supposed to know what to say, and how she was supposed to know if her plea had even been heard? She called out again—louder, desperate for help, any help at all.

Suddenly the phrase *Find your enemy's weakness and use it against him* popped into Cassidy's head. Where had she heard these words? *The enemy's weakness!* James had read about it in the book about the plague ghost!

Cassidy strained to remember the rest of the passage: *Chuan Lei was once a mortal himself who was almost as powerful as a dragon, but he became greedy and used his strength for evil purposes.*

It was his greediness that finally defeated him, she realized, still spinning wildly in the watery twister. *So how can I use that weakness against him?*

A plan began forming in her head, and she knew that it was now or never if she was going to make it work.

"I'll give you twelve children!" she shouted above the thundering din. The swirling slowed and then stopped. The waters of the lake began to settle into a slower boil, and she began treading the icy water. *I've gotten his attention.*

"I can bring you twelve children if you'll stop flooding the city and let me go," she said in as calm a voice as she could manage. She had to make him believe her or the plan would never work. She was counting on his interest in bargaining.

"You lie!" he shrieked, but Cassidy could tell that the promise of twelve children delivered into his watery depths tempted him. *His greed will be his downfall!*

"I'm not lying," she said, wondering how she could fight what was essentially a misty force. And then it occurred to her. *If he can change himself into a watery hand at my bedroom window or a hideous watery swirl, then maybe he can change into human form as well.* "But you have to disguise yourself as an old man—an old, white-haired grandfather. That way the kids will trust you. We can walk into the preschool and lead the children right out."

Around her the water curled and rolled and slapped against the steel supports of the bridge. She sensed the plague ghost making a decision. Wing Chun had taught her to anticipate her enemy's next move. She needed to be ready.

"You'll need me," she said calmly. "The children won't follow you unless I'm with you."

She began swimming slowly over to a large flat concrete slab under the bridge. *Is he buying this?* she wondered.

From the corner of her eye she could see the swirling mist of the plague ghost as he moved through the water toward her.

Greed, she said to herself. *Keep reminding him of what he could have.* "Twelve children," she said as she climbed out of the water and onto the slab. She stood up, shaking from the icy water and from fear. "All for you," she said. "They'll follow you right off the edge of the bridge."

Please let this work, she thought as she watched his watery form rise up from the churning lake and stand before her. Out of the water, he was a towering figure with yellow-green skin and a long white beard. His hair flowed around his face and down his shoulders and seemed to be in constant motion. His ropy tendrils reached out toward her as if they were alive.

"If you're lying to me," he roared in a voice that sounded as if it came from the darkest depths of the sea, "I can guarantee that your body will never be found!"

Cassidy had a terrifying vision of a future in which her parents grieved, never knowing what had really happened to her. They would assume that she had been swept into the lake, but they would always wonder. She couldn't let that happen. *I have to make this work. This is my only chance.*

"Now show me how you look as a grandfather," she said, surprised that her voice concealed the panic she felt inside.

The transformation started at his feet and moved up. Cassidy watched as the transparent, watery mist began to swirl and then thicken as he changed into a solid human form.

In a matter of seconds a stoop-shouldered old man stood before Cassidy, wearing a greenish gray rain slicker and boots. His white hair and beard, shorter now, curled around his face, and he looked as if he could be anybody's grandfather, except that his eyes were still the color of nothing.

"That's good," she said, taking a deep breath, willing herself to keep calm. "Very believable." Cassidy knew that he was the most human he could probably be and that this was the moment he would be the most vulnerable.

"Let's go," she said. "I'll take you to the children." He took a step forward, and Cassidy noticed how uncomfortable and awkward he seemed out of the water. *Even better*, Cassidy thought, sensing that the time had come to attack.

Before she turned, she positioned her fingertips to use as a weapon. She turned slowly, gracefully even, but when she struck, she hit the plague ghost hard and fast, forcefully jabbing him in the neck. *The movements of the crane are soft and flowing, but when he attacks, he exhibits a sudden burst of power*, she remembered from one of Master Lau's drills.

The plague ghost was caught off guard by the sudden attack. He brought his hands to his neck, making a watery gurgling noise deep in his throat. His eyes registered pain and surprise, but more than that, Cassidy noticed, his entire face burned with anger and hatred.

She made her second move before he had a chance to strike back—a quick series of painful jabs to his middle, disrupting his equilibrium. *Control your opponent's center of gravity* was another of Master Lau's lessons that Cassidy had learned but had never imagined she would actually use.

As Cassidy circled the plague ghost, preparing

for the third strike, she watched him sway. He was trying to regain his balance, but she also saw that something was happening to his form. The plague ghost was attempting to return to a watery mist. This time the change began at his head and moved down to his feet. Before the transformation was complete, Cassidy attacked one last time, knowing that this would likely be her last chance.

She spun quickly and brought her leg around. Her bent foot connected with the back of his knee. His legs buckled beneath him and he slammed forward. His semihuman form hit the concrete slab with a sickening thud.

Before Cassidy's eyes, the half-watery plague ghost began to dissolve. *What's happening?* Cassidy wondered. *Is he changing back? Is he going to rise up more angry and powerful than ever?* She circled the quickly disappearing form, her hands poised, ready to attack if she had to. An acid green pool sizzled into the concrete where the plague ghost had fallen. And then, as the ghost's remaining power drained away, the boiling water turned to nothing more than a greenish brown puddle. Cassidy watched as a gentle slap of blue lake water washed over the concrete, sweeping the murky puddle away.

"Cassidy, what are you doing?" Eliza called frantically from the far edge of the bridge, beyond the fallen and broken tree. *How long has Eliza been there?*

How much has she seen? Cassidy, her heart racing, began a climb up the bank toward the street above her, where her friend waited. Eliza's wet hair clung to her face, and she shivered from the cold.

"Did Sebastian make it back okay?" Cassidy asked, breathing heavily.

"Sebastian's fine," Eliza said with a look on her face that Cassidy couldn't read. "You, however, you don't look so fine. What was going on down there?"

So she did see something. "I fell in," Cassidy said, aware again of how thin the line was between the truth and a lie.

Eliza continued to look at Cassidy. "You fell in—that's it?"

"Look at me, Eliza," Cassidy said. "I'm soaking wet! You don't think I decided to just go for a swim, do you?"

"No, I believe you were in the water," Eliza said. "It's just that when I got up here, it looked like you were . . . I don't even know exactly, but it sort of looked like you were in the middle of a fight."

"A fight?" Cassidy asked, waiting before she said any more to determine just exactly what Eliza had seen.

"Yeah," Eliza said. "Oh, Cassidy, all right, I'll tell you. It looked like you were fighting an old man, okay? A really old man. And then when I got up here to the bridge, I didn't see him anymore."

Cassidy began to laugh. She was wet and exhausted and completely unsure about what was going on in her life, but the look on Eliza's face as she accused Cassidy of fighting an old man was too much.

"You saw me fighting an old man, Eliza?" Cassidy said. "I'm sorry, I'm not laughing at you . . . but it's just so . . ."

To Cassidy's relief, Eliza began laughing, too. "Luis was right," Eliza said. "It must be this rain! It's making everybody crazy! It's even making me see crazy things!"

And in that moment, Cassidy and Eliza realized that the rain had actually stopped. The ominous dark clouds that had covered the city for so long began to clear. Hanging low in the western sky, a brilliant sun shot dazzling orange and yellow streaks across Seattle.

🌸 Chapter Twenty-Three

"You could have drowned!" Wendy shrieked after Cassidy explained what happened. She had told her mother that she fell into the lake after the maintenance bridge broke away in the high wind and waves. She left out any mention of the plague ghost, of course.

Sebastian ran to Cassidy and wrapped his arms around her knees. "I'm okay, Mom," she said, patting the top of Sebastian's head. "I'm soaking wet, but I'm fine."

"Eliza, take her in the back," Wendy said, peeling Sebastian off Cassidy's legs. "There's an old paint smock and some other clothes back there, Cassidy. Dry off and get warm."

Sebastian was squealing for her. "Cassidy, where the puppy go?"

"Hey, buddy, I don't know. I guess the puppy went home," she said, bending over to see him better.

"Where monster?" Sebastian asked.

"Monster?" Cassidy said. "I don't know what you're talking about."

"Sebastian came running into the day care," Eliza said, "yelling something about a water monster."

"The lake was churning, you know, with the rain and the wind. I guess it looked like a monster to him," Cassidy said.

"Go dry off, change clothes," Cassidy's mother said. "Or the *bad-cold* monster will get you."

"Sure, Mom," Cassidy said, laughing, but somehow she knew that she wouldn't get sick from being in the freezing water. In fact, she had never felt better.

Eliza helped Mrs. Chen with the parents' pickup while Cassidy dried off in the back. She changed into an old pair of sweatpants with rainbow-colored specks of paint all over them. On another hook she found a thick, woolly, oatmeal-colored sweater that her mother wore on cold days at the Happy Bunny.

"And now modeling the latest fashions from Paris is Cassidy Chen, wearing an original Happy Bunny ensemble!" Cassidy strutted runway style into the large open room where Wendy and Eliza were putting away art supplies.

"Ooh la la," her mother said with a laugh.

"Yeah, and here's something from one of your adoring fans." Eliza handed Cassidy a piece of art paper. Around the edge of the paper Sebastian had scribbled furious curls of white water, and at the center he had colored a green face with an open mouth and hollow eyes.

"That was a very brave thing you did today," Simon said at dinner that evening. "When your mother called and told me what had . . . well, I don't even want to think about what could have happened out there, but I know you were thinking about the little boy."

"Oh, Dad, I didn't do anything, not really," Cassidy said, wondering how much longer she could keep her secret from her parents.

"You were thinking about the safety of someone else and you acted on it. That's courage, Cassidy. That's being brave," her dad said.

She thought about the way she had hung on to Sebastian and to the steel cable at the same time. *How was I able to do that? I'm not that strong. And how was I able to hold my breath for so long when I was underwater?* Then she thought about the way she had healed so quickly after she'd defeated the winged snake—*Maybe the gift also makes me stronger somehow.*

She remembered calling out to her ancestors for help. *Right after I called on them, I thought of the plan to trick the plague ghost. Did my ancestors really hear me? Something happened out there—something beyond what I could have done on my own.*

Cassidy realized she had fought the plague ghost using Wing Chun techniques that she had practiced only a few times. And she was pretty sure that the last move, the powerful kick that had finally brought down the plague ghost, was just a technique she'd seen in a movie once.

Cassidy sensed that a shift had begun to take place in her relationship with her parents. *I've changed. I know in my bones that I've changed. And maybe Mom and Dad sense that, too.*

"You're growing up so fast, Cassidy," her mother said. And that's when Cassidy realized her mother and father saw only that she was changing from their little girl into a young woman.

They don't really know I'm becoming more than that, Cassidy thought. *Do I even know? I've fought two demons now—and won! What does that make me? A warrior, like the women in the dream said?*

Cassidy wondered how much she could tell her

mom and dad about what was happening to her. *Should I try? Maybe test the water and see what they say?*

"Remember those coins?" Cassidy began. "Well, what if they brought some kind of danger, maybe some evil that had to be fought . . ." She stopped and tried to read her parents' faces. *Do they think I'm crazy?*

Her father cleared his throat before speaking. "What kind of danger or evil are you talking about, Cassidy?"

"I don't know . . . but, well, all the rain—the storms—for example," she said. "The streets were flooding. . . . it was really bad."

"Rain is natural, Cassidy," her mother said. "We certainly had more than our share, but it's over now. Are you saying you think the coins had something to do with the rain?"

Cassidy didn't know how to answer. Could she say, *Yes, I think the rain was caused by the plague ghost, an ancient, evil spirit who causes floods. I had to fight him—I had to defeat him to get the rain to stop. And not only that, I think the winged snake was a demon and he was making me sick by poisoning me somehow. I had to defeat him, too!*

"Do you want us to get rid of the coins?" Simon asked her. "Are you afraid of them?"

"No, Dad," Cassidy said quickly. "I'm not afraid of them."

"Is there something else bothering you, Cass?" her mom asked. "Something you want to talk about?"

But Cassidy knew that the time just wasn't right. She wanted to tell them what had happened, but it would have to wait. Maybe she needed some time to understand it more herself before she could share it with anybody else.

"It was just a question, that's all," Cassidy said in a much lighter tone. "You know . . . like, what if the coins are cursed by some demons and they have to be fought . . . like a good-versus-evil kind of thing."

"Oh, like a book or movie?" Wendy asked.

"Yeah, exactly," Cassidy replied.

"Sounds like a great idea for a story," her father told her. "Maybe you should put that imagination of yours to use and write it down!"

ଚ୍ଚ୍ଚ୍ଚ୍ଚ

The phone rang after dinner. "Okay, I *know* it's too late to call, so don't kill me, but I've got to tell you this," Eliza said as Cassidy picked up the phone. "Guess who my mom went out with tonight? She just got back like fifteen minutes ago."

"The guy at the shipping place where she drops off her packages?" Cassidy asked. Sarah Clifford had said she thought he looked like an older Brad Pitt, which gave Cassidy and Eliza quite a laugh.

"No, not the Brad clone," Eliza said. "You'll never guess, so I'll have to tell you—Patrick Healy!"

"You mean Patrick Healy, the Healer? How could I forget?" *He's the one who picked up on the snake demon's curse long before I did, after all.* "I thought she decided that he was a quack and that she didn't like him because he kept asking her out."

"You know my mom," Eliza said. "Maybe she just changed her mind about him, but anyway, they went out and she told me she had a great time. She's invited him over for *dinner* this weekend. But here's the best part. When I asked her if she was sure she wanted to start something a month before we were supposed to leave, she just said, 'Oh, I don't know; it's awfully hot in Phoenix.'"

"Told you she'd change her mind," Cassidy said. "Probably because it finally stopped raining today."

"Exactly! That rain was like some kind of curse, you know? I'm glad it's over. Everything's just been so . . . weird lately. I hope it stops."

❧❧❧❧❧

Later, back in her room, Cassidy sat on her bed and closed her eyes, trying to absorb everything that had happened. *Eliza was right—everything has been unbelievably weird lately.* After a moment she got up and took out the box of coins. She wasn't surprised to find that the wave coin was warm to the touch. She held it tightly and let its warmth flow gently into her hand.

"We were with you at the bridge today."

Cassidy looked up and saw the shimmering image of an older woman standing before her. Her curly red hair, streaked with gray, was piled on top of her head. Her eyes were a brilliant shamrock green that perfectly matched the long full dress she wore. The woman's presence brought warmth to the room that wrapped Cassidy in comfort and took away any fear that seeing a stranger appear might bring.

But she's not a stranger, she realized, *she's one of my ancestors! This is my mother's grandmother—the one who sprinkled her with the fairy dust when she was little!*

My mother's grandmother? When Cassidy called on her ancestors for help, she'd thought about the ancestors from the Chinese side of her family.

"Oh, don't look so surprised, my darling," the woman said with a lilting Irish accent. "The emerald green hills of our mother country hide spirits in their pale mist. Why, there's magic under the gnarled roots of every tree in Ireland, sweetheart! And you, my precious one, have been sprinkled with destiny's own golden dust!"

From the shadows of Cassidy's room stepped three other spirits that stood before her like luminous figures of light. Cassidy tried to let her eyes adjust to the brightness brought into the room when the spirits appeared, but it was almost impossible. She could see that there was one other woman who appeared to be

Chinese and two men, but they didn't seem to be as clearly formed as her Irish great-grandmother. "This is your gift," her great-grandmother said, indicating the other spirits in the room. "We have always been here, but now you'll be able to see us. Your Chinese ancestors call this the 'gift of Yin.' And we Irish call it 'second sight.'"

"The gift of Yin? Second sight?" Cassidy asked. "Do you mean . . . ? Are you ghosts?"

"We're friendly spirits who care a great deal for you. You called on us for help today, and that pleased us very much."

"And you helped me," Cassidy said. "That's how I was able to defeat the plague ghost?"

"You did it, sweet girl. We only offered encouragement and love."

Cassidy thought about this. These four wonderful people who were her ancestors had strengthened her, had guided her so that she would know what to do. *James was so right,* she realized.

"How come the others aren't speaking?" Cassidy asked. "Why am I able to see you better than them?"

The woman laughed, and it sounded like bells to Cassidy's ears. "Oh, it's a true mystery and difficult to explain!" she said. "There's a thin veil between the two worlds. Perhaps I'm able to push through that veil a bit stronger now, but it's not always that way. The energy ebbs and flows—like the energy of life!"

"So, I can see you whenever I want?" Cassidy asked.

"You'll always be aware of our presence—and occasionally you'll see us or hear us as well. Not just us, but perhaps other spirits, too. Some, I'm afraid, not as friendly. Let your eyes show you what you know in your heart is true—this is also the gift of Yin—this is also second sight."

"Can you tell me why this is happening?" Cassidy asked. "Why I've had to fight two demons?"

"As I said, this is your destiny. But you know that already, don't you? Your Chinese ancestors were true warriors—they've visited you in dreams."

"Yes, but I don't understand why!" Cassidy said. "Everything started when I got the coins. Are the coins even meant for me?"

"Yes, dear one, the coins have always been meant for you. Your ancestors Wing Chun and Ng Mui told you as much. Use them well."

"That was written on the note," Cassidy said.

"Yes, my child, it was. We must go now," her great-grandmother said. "Your sweet mother is on her way."

Wendy Chen knocked lightly at Cassidy's door just as the four spirits began to fade. In the absence of their brilliant light, the room seemed dim—cold, even.

"Are you still up?" her mother called softly.

Cassidy opened her door. "I was just looking at the coins."

Wendy came into the room and then stopped suddenly. She had a peculiar look on her face. "Strange," she said, and then sniffed the air. "Do you smell that perfume?"

"What do you mean, Mom?" Cassidy asked.

"When I was a little girl, I would sit in my grandmother Fiona's lap and she would read to me. She always smelled like lavender. That's what I smell now."

Cassidy also detected a light whiff of lavender in the room but didn't mention it. "That's a nice memory, Mom," she said, feeling more at peace than she had in a long time.

🏵 Chapter Twenty-Four

Cassidy read for a while and then went downstairs to get a glass of milk before going to bed. Wendy and Simon were at the table, which was covered with old photo albums and boxes of loose pictures and knickknacks.

"Come here, Cassidy," Wendy said. "Look at this." She flipped through the yellowed pages and pointed to a small snapshot. "This is a picture of my grandmother. That lavender scent got me thinking about all these old photos."

Cassidy studied the picture. This was the same

woman who had appeared in her room.

"That's so cool, Mom," Cassidy said. "I've never seen any of these pictures." Cassidy turned a few more pages filled with pictures of large family gatherings, children standing in front of Christmas trees and posed on the backs of ponies.

Wendy pulled something from one of the boxes. "I want you to have this," she said. "It was my grandmother's."

Cassidy took a dark tortoiseshell comb from her mother's hand and examined it. Along the top was an elaborate carving of feathers, dotted with small green stones.

"It's beautiful, Mom," Cassidy said. "Thanks."

"I'm not expecting you to wear it or anything—I kind of doubt it's the fashion statement you want to make."

Cassidy laughed and held it up to her hair. "Oh, I don't know. I think it's kind of glamorous!"

"She was an amazing woman. I remember the stories she told about beautiful fairies that would fly up to my window at night and look in at me—she said they wanted to see what a real girl looked like. And then there were the stories of terrible trolls and evil goblins! The way she described them made you think she'd actually seen them with her own eyes!"

"Maybe she had," Cassidy said.

Wendy laughed. "I guess you're right. Maybe

she had."

Simon picked up the other photo album. He began turning the pages. "We should do something with these," he said. "They're not very well preserved, just stuck away on a shelf somewhere."

"You could scan them, Dad," Cassidy suggested. "At least you'd have a digital copy then."

"That's a good idea. That'll be my next project," he said. "Maybe we can work on it together."

Simon pointed to a photograph and laughed. "I look like such a little nerd in this picture."

Cassidy looked at her father as a small boy in short pants and dark glasses. His black hair was combed severely to one side. He was holding his mother's hand, and he seemed to be squinting at the camera. "You were so cute, Dad," Cassidy said.

Simon shook his head and turned the page. Cassidy looked over his shoulder at the next picture. It was a black and white photograph of a thin, youngish man in a white starched shirt and dark pleated pants. He was standing on the corner of a narrow street in San Francisco. Cassidy could see a portion of the Golden Gate Bridge in the distance behind him.

Cassidy frowned. *I've seen this man before.* A vision swam before Cassidy's eyes: *An older man stands in the fog. He sees her and he bows his head slightly. A wisp of hair falls across his forehead—a streak of pure white hair against the gray. He pushes his hair out of his face, and then he hands her a box.*

"I think that might be him," Cassidy said, pulling her chair over to get a closer look at the picture. "I think that's the man who gave me the box of coins on my birthday. He had a streak of white in his hair just like that."

"That's actually not possible," Simon said. "That's my father. He died when I was . . . well, when I was your age."

"It was a boating accident, wasn't it, Simon?" Wendy asked, looking at the photograph of the handsome young man.

"Yes, he went fishing one day and didn't come back. His overturned boat was found about a week later."

Cassidy looked closely at the photograph. There was no mistaking the streak of pure white that began at his right temple, angling back like a white feather against the man's black hair.

It was him, Cassidy was almost certain of it. The question was whether he was alive or a ghost.

ഗ൧ഗ൧ഗ

"Shake a leg, Cassidy, my dear," her mother said as she raised the blinds in Cassidy's bedroom the following morning. "Is this not a beautiful day or what?"

"You're sure feeling good today," Cassidy said.

"Dad and I are taking a day off; can you believe it?" Wendy said. "I called in *gone* today. Now that the weather's cleared, June and Carol can both make it in to the preschool. I told them they owed me big time after yesterday."

At the breakfast table, Simon Chen had stacked a plate high with muffins. He sat relaxed at one end of the table with the newspaper open in front of him. "So what's the plan, Dad?" Cassidy asked.

"Mom and I are going to the art museum this morning, and then I think we'll have a late lunch at the Dahlia."

"Ooh, the Dahlia," said Cassidy. "And I guess I'll be stuck at school eating, oh, I don't know—if I'm lucky, maybe fish sticks and lime Jell-O." Cassidy smiled at the idea of a plain old normal school day.

She slung her backpack over her shoulder and then grabbed a muffin off the table. "I'm meeting Eliza down at the corner. You two have a reasonable amount of fun today."

The world looked washed clean in the brilliant sunshine. Cassidy stood on her front stoop and took it all in—from the noisy chorus of seabirds to the craggy peaks of the distant mountains, white with snow. The bare trees on her street glistened silver against the sapphire sky, and the cleansing scent of evergreens filled her senses with the kind of purity that comes from newness—from fresh starts and new days.

She looked toward the end of the drive and remembered the morning of her birthday, when the man with the white streak in his hair had given her the box of coins. *Are those coins really meant to help me fulfill my destiny as a warrior princess?*

Cassidy wondered what it would sound like to actually say the words out loud. "I am Mingmei. I am a warrior princess."

Well, that doesn't sound so bad, she thought. *In fact, it sounded kind of . . . okay.*

Glancing down the street, Cassidy saw Eliza turn the corner and wave her arms wildly. Eliza pointed to her head. *Is her hair—pink today? She must be celebrating something—maybe she's celebrating the possible nonmove to Phoenix!*

She waved to Eliza and thought how great it was to have a best friend with pink hair, to have parents who were playing hooky, and to have James as . . . well, she didn't know what James was yet— maybe her friend, maybe something else, something a little more . . . interesting. . . . Or maybe as the ally her dream had foretold? *Maybe,* she thought. *But I don't need an ally today. I'm not ready to be a warrior princess today. Today I'm Cassidy Chen.*